# ARK

# J.J. WILDER

# FOREWORD

The story of the Great Flood as told in Genesis chapters 6–8 is one that has long fascinated me. The details were so few, and as a child my vivid imagination left me wondering what it must have been like to be Noah, or one of his sons, to build this enormous boat completely on faith, to watch animals come seemingly of their own accord, to witness Earth flood. I wondered, and I wondered, and I wondered, and finally, I decided to put my imagination to work and explore the story by trying to write it.

Another aspect that has always intrigued me occurs within a few sentences in Genesis chapter 6 that hint at a culture of half-angels, the bastard children of other-than humans who once walked this earth. Known as the Nephilim, I have always wondered about them and their society, at their world so deviant, so vile, so violent that it was wiped away wholesale.

Ancient cultures such as the Sumerians, the proto-Chinese of the Far East, South American peoples, the aborigines of Australia, and the great seafaring races in the islands of Indonesia all have oral and written stories of a great flood. Historical, geological, and archeological records all bear out this story. What's more, these records and stories are *all* from the same general epoch, which just happens to coincide with the timeline set out in the book of Genesis.

This is not a religious novel; it isn't even necessarily spiritual. It is a fantasy, a fictional novel placed in an historical setting, within the context of a Biblical story. It is not meant to inform anyone's beliefs, to challenge anyone's worldviews, nor is it attempting to communicate a larger message. Don't believe in a worldwide flood? That's OK. Then consider this story nothing more than fantasy, like *Game of Thrones* or *Lord of the Rings*.

Whatever you believe I hope you enjoy reading this book because it is, and has been and will continue to be, a fascinating story for me.

# GLOSSARY OF NAMES AND TERMS

**TERMS and PLACES**

**Cubit**: an ancient unit of measurement, equal to 1.5 feet. (Pronunciation: *CYOO-bit*)

**Nephilim**: a race of people mentioned in the Bible as being the resulting offspring when angels took human women as wives; Nephilim are described as the "mighty men of old, heroes of renown." My physical description of them is purely fictional and imaginative. My placement of them in the context of Sumerian history is also fictional, and a literary liberty. If the Nephilim were real, they probably would have predated even Sumerian society, which was merely the first culture to produce cities for which we have ruins and records, rather than the first true culture or society. It is entirely possible, if you ask me, that there were earlier cultures for whom no record exists, and left no ruins for us to find. (Pronunciation: NEH-fih-leem)

**Sappara**: a real weapon used in ancient times. It is similar to an axe, being primarily a chopping weapon. The Egyptians used a similar weapon called a *khopesh;* the sappara was only sharpened on the convex side, meaning the outer side of the curve, whereas the Egyptian *khopesh* was sharpened on both sides. (Pronunciation: *SAH-pah-rah)*

**Onager**: A species of ass or donkey native to Asia and the Middle East. (Pronunciation: *OHN-ahj-er*)

**Aurochs**: an animal like an oxen, only much, much larger, now extinct. (Pronunciation: *Awr-ox*)

**Bad-Tibira**: A real, historical Sumerian city. There are physical ruins in Iraq, southeast of Baghdad and northwest of Basrah, but my descriptions of the city are fictional and products of my imagination; the other cities mentioned in this book are also historical locations, all located mostly in modern day Iraq. (Pronunciation: *Bad Tih-BEER-ah*)

**Anu, Ereshkigal, Inanna, Ninurta, Enil, etc.**: gods of the Sumerian pantheon. There are too many to list or describe here, and many of them have several names and appear in the pantheons of similar or related cultures, such as the Akkadians and Babylonians. Wikepedia has an extensive section on Sumerian gods, for those interested. The gods of this epoch are so vast in number that they make the pantheons of the Greeks and Romans seem minuscule in comparison.

**Kur**: the Sumerian underworld. (Pronunciation: *Koor*)

**Ziggurat**: A stepped pyramid, common in Sumerian, Akkadian, Babylonian, and similar cultures. Also found in South America and other early civilizations.


**PEOPLE**

**Aresia**: The only daughter and youngest child of King Emmen-Utu; a Nephilim. (Pronunciation: *Ah-REE-zee-ya*)

**Japheth**: Oldest son of Noah; a human. He is mentioned in the Bible, but there is no indication as to the birth order of Noah's sons, so making him the eldest is a bit of a literary liberty on my part. (Pronunciation: *JAY-feth*)

**Noah**: Japheth's father, builder of the ark. (Pronunciation: NO-ah)

**Emmen-Utu**: King of Bad-Tibira, Aresia's father; a Nephilim. He is a real, historical figure, although in historical records his name is En-men-lu-ana, or Emmen-Luana; I changed his name to sound more masculine to modern readers. (Pronunciation: EH-men OO-too)

**Irkalla**: Aresia's maidservant, and only friend; a Nephilim. (Pronunciation: *Ihr-KAH-lah)*

**Kichu**: Oldest son of King Emmen-Utu, crown prince of Bad-Tibira; a Nephilim; not a historical figure. (Pronunciation: *KEE-choo*).

**Dummuzi**: A son of Emmen-Utu; not a historical figure; a Nephilim. (Pronunciation: *Doo-MOO-zee)*

**Algar**: A son of Emmen-Utu; not a historical figure; a Nephilim. (Pronunciation: *AL-gar)*
**Immuru**: A son of Emmen-Utu; not a historical figure; a Nephilim. (Pronunciation: *ee-MOO-roo)*

**Zin-Suddu**: A son of Emmen-Utu; not a historical figure; a Nephilim. (Pronunciation: *Zin SOO-doo)*

**Zara**: Noah's wife, Japheth's mother. Only the men are mentioned by name in the Bible, so she is a fictional character; a human. (Pronunciation: *ZA-rah)*

**Neses**: betrothed to Japheth; daughter of Namus; a fictional character; a human. (Pronunciation: *NEH-seez)*

**Sedele**: Shem's wife; daughter of Namus, Neses's and Sedele's sister; a fictional character; a human. (Pronunciation: *SEH-deh-lah)*

**Ne'eletama**: Ham's wife; daughter of Namus, Neses's and Sedele's sister; a fictional character; a human. (Pronunciation: *NEH-leh-tah-mah*)

**Enkidu**: personal bodyguard to Emmen-Utu, captain of the king's personal guard; a Nephilim. (Pronunciation: *Enk-EE-doo*)

**Sin-Iddim**: a real, historical king of Larsa; his name is also rendered Sin-Idnim; a Nephilim. (Pronunciation: *Sin id-EEM*)

**Zidan**: Japheth's best friend, and a fellow mercenary and warrior; a human. (Pronunciation: *ZEE-dahn*)

**Urugan**: a human merchant. (Pronunciation: *oo-rooh-GAHN*)

**Mesh-te**: High Priest of Ereshkigal in the city of Ur; a Nephilim. (Pronunciation: *Mesh TEY*)

**Argandea**: King of Uruk, a fictional character; a Nephilim. (Pronunciation: ahr-GAHN-dee-yah)

**Lugash**: A general from Larsa; a Nephilim. (Pronunciation: *LOO-gash*)

**Mirra**: a healer in the city of Larsa; a Nephilim. (Pronunciation: *MEER-ah*)

**Sannin**: a Nephilim male mentioned by Mirra. (Pronunciation: *San-in*)

**Jorin**: a Nephilim male mentioned by Mirra (Pronunciation: *JORE-in)*

**Dagan**: General from Larsa; a Nephilim. (Pronunciation: *Dah-gahn*)

**Amar**: Crown prince of Uruk, slain in battle by Japheth. (Pronunciation: *Ah-MAR*)

**Uresh**: a warrior of Larsa; a Nephilim. (Pronunciation: *YOOR-esh*)

**Namus**: Noah's business partner, transported crops from Noah's farm to Bad-Tibira; Neses's father; a human. (Pronunciation: NAY-muss)

# ARK

# CHAPTER 1

## Nephilim

"... The sons of God saw that the daughters
of men were beautiful; and they took wives
for themselves, whomever they chose ... the
Nephilim were on the earth in those days ...
those were the might men who were of old,
men of renown." Genesis 6:2–4 (NASB)

*Bad-Tibira, Ancient Sumer, circa 2400 B.C.*

NORMALLY, THE FEEL OF THE BRUSH RUNNING
through my hair was relaxing. It was always
the last thing my maidservant, Irkalla, did for me
before I retired to my bed. The soothing strokes
through my glossy auburn hair, Irkalla's quick, sure
fingers dancing and tugging and untangling, her
voice often lilting in some song, a lullaby or a hymn

to Inanna . . . I was frequently half asleep before Irkalla even finished.

Not tonight.

Tonight, nothing could relax me. I could not eat, could not sit still, and could not stop my fingers fidgeting. My rooms were close to the throne room, which meant even with the doors pulled shut I could hear the cries and screams and pleas of Father's latest prisoner. I sat in that throne room tonight, attempting to appear unaffected by the ugliness and gore, and the screams as the human prisoners begged for mercy or for death. Tonight, I could not do it any longer, and I begged my father to excuse me. Yet even back in my rooms, there is little escape, for I can still hear him.

"Highness," Irkalla said, "Forgive me, but . . . you aren't yourself this evening."

"How can I be, Irkalla?" I waved a hand toward the throne room. "Father has another human prisoner. I hate this. He's had the poor creature for days."

She tugged the brush gently through the tangle, loosening the snarl until the brush swept through easily once more. "I know. It's terrible. Small mercy it may be, but I heard one of the guards saying the prisoner won't last the night." She stroked through my hair a few more times. "Perhaps I could bring you a sleeping draught in some wine?"

I nodded. "Very well."

I stood up, examining myself in my polished bronze mirror. My auburn hair fell in long, smooth, glossy tresses down around my shoulders, wavering around my elbows. My eyes glowed golden, like all Nephilim's eyes did, and my skin was faintly luminous as well, a golden shimmer as if the radiance of the sun burned within me, somehow. Clad in only a thin shift, my body was clearly visible, my hips, my trim waist, my generous bust. I knew men considered me beautiful—among Nephilim men it was generally accepted that I was the most beautiful woman in Bad-Tibira, and those few humans who have looked upon me and left the palace alive, well . . . to them, I am a goddess.

I could see Irkalla behind me, still fully clothed in a servant's plain dress. Despite the roughspun nature of her garments, Irkalla was very nearly as beautiful as I, or so whispered the other servants and guards. She was truly lovely, with golden hair the color of sunlight on wheat, fair skin with only a faint shimmer of Nephilim luminosity, and wide, expressive eyes whose golden glow was muted by her lineage—the more human ancestry a Nephilim possessed in his or her bloodline, the more muted the glow. Irkalla was striking, with sharp features, a strong bearing, and a generous figure. Suitable, I supposed, for a maidservant to a princess.

She smiled at me in our reflection and then

swept gracefully from the room to prepare my sleeping draught. I settled myself in my bed, but I was still restless and discomfited. I doubted even with the herbs to hasten sleep I would find much rest.

Despite the sleeping draught, the screams kept me awake. The prisoner kept calling on Elohim to help him, to save him, but Elohim was silent, and his pitiful pleas to The One God only enraged my father all the more. I wished I could go to the poor prisoner and tell him he might find release in death, if only he would cease his cries to The One God.

My father hated Elohim. He hated any mention of His Name, and the prisoner only ensured the worsening of his torture by his ceaseless yowling of that hated name. If he had called on our gods, on Enki or Inanna, Father might have ended his pain with one swift blow to the head.

When finally the prisoner fell silent and went to meet his One God, I was relieved.

It was late and still sleep did not come. As I lay among my pillows and gazed out the window at the stars above, my mind began to drift and, unaccountably, I thought of my father.

As a powerful Nephilim king, Father hated humans. Compared to our race, he said, they were short and small and weak. He held their brief lives in contempt, and claimed that anyone who did not live at least 200 years was no better than an animal. We, the Nephilim, sons and daughters born when the gods mated with humans, were extraordinarily tall of stature and long-lived—men stood at least five cubits tall, and we women four and half, and we lived many, many hundreds of years, whereas the tallest human male stood shorter than even the most stooped old crone, barely clearing four cubits at most, and most of them died after a hundred years, if not less.

Father said humankind did not deserve the earth, and so he relieved them of it, one person at a time. He was not a kind man, my father the king. The name of King Emmen-Utu was known far and wide, spoken with respect and whispered in fear. Even the other Nephilim Kings treated him gingerly, stepping carefully in his presence.

As his daughter, it was no different for me. He was no kinder as a father than he was as a king.

My brothers were of little help. They were strangers, mostly, all of them much older than I. As men and royals, they were busy with war and politics and bedding women. I had five brothers: Kichu, Algar, Immuru, Zin-Suddu, and Dummuzi. Algar and Immuru were generals in Father's army, leading raids against other cities and defending our borders. Dummuzi, as the youngest, was still in training, and thus lived in the soldier's barracks.

Only Kichu, as the eldest and thus crown prince, was ever nearby, and it was he to whom I was closest. His rooms were near mine, and he was often about helping Father run the city and resolve arguments. Wandering around the palace during the day, I often saw him in a garden or in the hallways, and we might have walked together, chatting amiably.

I wish I could have said I loved my father, the king. The sad truth, however, was that I hated him. Every night I laid my head to the pillow and said a prayer to Enki and to Inanna, and I asked them to strike him down in his sleep.

Alas, they were callous gods, and did not heed the cries of mere mortals such as I, even a Nephilim and the daughter of a king.

My father might not have loved me, and he might not have doted on me, or showered me with gifts, but at the least, he did not confine me to my rooms, and he had not married me off to some fat old King in a far-flung corner of the land. He had threatened it many times when I'd angered him, but I think he secretly regretted and still mourned the death of my mother, and he kept me around as a kind of penance. If Father and my brothers were any example of husbands, I wanted nothing more than to live alone.

But the suitors kept coming.

Inanna spare me, they came in droves. Burly,

swaggering, hairy hulks, all of them, weighed down with gold and silver and jewels, swinging their spears and scratching their groins and grunting like apes. They stormed the palace, ate our food and drank our wine and tumbled the palace whores, and then they had the gall to try and woo me with the whore's kohl still smeared on their faces. I would have rather been hung from the palace gates than to marry one of them.

My only refuge was out beyond the palace walls, down near the temple and among the rabble and the humans. They fascinated me, these short-statured and short-lived men and women. They scurried about like mice fleeing storm waters, but they were resilient and determined. Even the poorest seemed to find more joy in the simplest of things than my father and brothers did in their fine clothes and expensive wines. Even the poorest of them were kinder than my people. They were weak, yes, and they lived lives as short as mice, but at least they treated each other with something like decency.

The palace was a high-walled monstrosity of kiln-baked brick occupying the center of Bad-Tibira. The walls extended hundreds and hundreds of cubits north to south, and it was half as wide as it was long. The walls of the palace itself stood a dozen cubits high and were wide enough that three men could walk abreast from watchtower to watchtower, which were spaced every twelve to fifteen cubits along the wall.

Within the walls was a maze of lush gardens and wide hallways and echoing chambers, and everywhere you looked there were knots of royal guards striding imperiously, hobnailed sandals cracking against the floor, spearheads glinting in the bright sun, and officials scurrying here and there alone and in twos and larger groups, conversing importantly and gesticulating and often shouting. Occasionally, courtiers and messengers and petitioners made their way inside from the palace gates situated across the mammoth echoing courtyard.

Once through the palace gates, you were faced with that courtyard, a gaping expanse of brick walkways and towering buildings to the left and to the right. Lines of stoic, unmoving, silent guards stood at each doorway. Groups of other guards marched in formation across the courtyard only to stop at one end and pivot to pace back.

Crossing that courtyard was an intimidating experience, with statues of Enlil and Inanna watching you, guards staring you down as if probing your soul for ill intent, your footsteps loud in your own ears, the courtyard so large it took minutes of walking to go from the outer gate to the inner gate.

The inner gate was a huge arch of hand-hewn

stone, heavy and imposing, carved with the likenesses of Utu the Sun God, and Lord Enlil and Lady Inanna. Three guards stood on either side of the gate, watching every step you took and every breath you drew. More guards stood on the inner walls, pacing the perimeter of the inner royal sanctum, bows drawn, arrows nocked.

Once through the inner gate you reached a mighty ramp wide enough for four chariots abreast, yet steep enough that it winded you to climb up. Up, and up, and up, to the towering walls of the throne room and the royal bedchambers and the kitchens, fierce stone-carved lions at each door and hard-eyed guards with razor sharp spears and gleaming swords standing guard.

The throne room occupied the center of the royal sanctum, with the King's chambers taking up the entire rightmost wing, my brothers' and my rooms on the left, each of us having our own servants' quarters. As well, our personal chambers contained dressing rooms and bathing rooms and nightsoil chambers, as well as guard's nooks and balconies and courtyards. The walls of our royal sanctum were hung with lavish tapestries, and the stone floors were covered in the finest rugs, and the rooms filled with gold-gilt statues of the gods and goddesses. The guards were clothed in the finest robes, their helms glittering with precious gems, their spear hafts polished to a gleam, their swords forged by the finest smiths in the kingdom.

Yet for all the lavish luxury, the palace often seemed like a prison to me. Guards watched my every step, whether I was in my own rooms, going to the temple of Inanna accompanied by Irkalla or to the throne room to sit with Father at ceremonial affairs, or taking the evening meal in the dining chambers.

The only freedom I ever found was in dressing in the plainest, coarsest, rough-spun robes and sneaking out of the palace with Irkalla. It was always a tense, fraught affair, my head kept down, my heart hammering as we tiptoed across the courtyard and out of the palace to the city beyond. If the guards knew me, they never stopped me, which might have been thanks in part to the glitter of gold passing from Irkalla's hand to theirs.

Even cloaked in a plain woolen robe so as not to draw attention, I could tell that they feared me, seeing my height and occasionally glimpsing my face. I thought some of them knew who I was, and thus offered me deference in fear of my father's wrath. If I could I would have told them that I would never betray them to him, but they would have only pleaded for mercy and trembled all the more, and that would have ruined my pleasure among them; thus I let them think what they will.

Even with the sleeping draught Irkalla gave me, sleep eluded me well into the smallest hours of the dawn, and it was late in the day when I finally arose and left my chambers. I waited until full dark that night to sneak out of the palace with Irkalla; if I had but known the trouble I would have finding sleep again that night, and why, I might have stayed in the palace.

Tonight Father was in his cups, and it was at such times when he was most dangerous, so I clothed myself in my plain commoner's robes and had Irkalla accompany me to my favorite temple, a tiny, rude little building far off the main road, hunched and crammed between taller, newer buildings, and overshadowed by a towering ziggurat to Enlil.

It was easy to miss, being dark within and as old as the stars themselves, the once-handsomely carved exterior long-since crumbled. I had discovered it by accident, one day, while lost with Irkalla, and I fell in love with it. It was nothing but four crumbling brick walls and a slab of stone across the top, the ceiling so low I felt the stone brushing my hair if I stood upright, and the walls were close and stained with age. This place had been there for an age already, and the altar to Inanna was a soot-stained block of stone with a rudely carved little statue to the goddess and a few guttering candles.

The priestess was as old as the temple, stooped and hunched and wrinkled, and though she knew me, she allowed me to come and pay my respects to the goddess and say a prayer or make an offering.

This night, however, was different. I was not here to make an offering to Inanna. It was the anniversary of my mother's death, and the reason for my Father's drunken rage, and my own steep melancholy. I lit a candle and wafted the smoke to the ceiling, whispered a prayer to my goddess, and tried to remember my mother. Tall, imperiously beautiful, her hair the same rich glossy auburn as my own, always left loose in a cascade around her shoulders and waist, her eyes kohled and her nostrils pierced and her ears hung with precious jewels, her wrists adorned with gold, the bracelets clattering as she walked and tinkling as she caught me up in her lithe arms.

I remembered her singing to me at night, teaching me prayers to Lady Inanna, showing me how to light the candle and waft the sweet smoke to the heavens. I remembered her sitting on her chair beside Father's throne: head high, a gold circlet on her brow. I remembered her lying beside me as I drifted to sleep, her skin smelling of perfume and her hair of jasmine.

I remembered, too, the night she died. I had heard a shout and stumbled from my bed to the doorway of the throne room. Father was lounging on his throne, and a naked human girl was on top of him, writhing sinuously and moaning loudly, her eyes hooded as if dazed by the herbs the priests used to commune with the gods.

Father had a wineskin in his hand, and Mother was standing in the center of the throne room, kohl dripping in black streaks down her cheeks. I remembered her cursing Father, calling him dog and pig, damning him in the vilest terms. I remember Father throwing the girl off of him, stumbling from the dais, and swinging his fist clumsily at Mother. Even a half-strength blow from my father was enough to fell an ox; a drunken strike such as that one . . . it connected with Mother's temple, cracking wetly, and she fell. I watched as she tumbled to the floor, and I watched as her head struck the stones with a sickening crunch, and then redness seeped out of her to stain the flags.

Father fell to his knees, cradling her, cursing her, cursing himself, begging her to get up, begging her to forgive him. I remembered the way Mother's head lolled oddly, dripping crimson. Father changed that night, and his distaste for humans soured further into open hatred and persecution.

I was much like my mother, so said Irkalla and the other servants, and I thought my face reminded Father of her, reminding him of his sin, of his guilt, of his shame. He sank deep into his cups and was prone to sudden and terrible rages, and gods help anyone who got in his way. He had been known to kill messengers and servants for the slightest transgression, and if there were any humans in the dungeons, they died awful deaths at his hand. And if I was near him, I received the worst of his rage. He did not strike me, but he cursed me, accosted me with epithets and threw things at me until I left.

Thus, on the anniversary of Mother's death I stayed in my rooms until it was dark and then I made my way to this temple, and I remembered Mother the best I could, whispering her name and calling up her face—a face that grew more hazy and distant with each passing year.

When I had lit my candle and said my prayers, when I had remembered my mother and offered propitiation to Inanna on my Mother's behalf, Irkalla and I scurried out of the temple and threaded our way through the dark, narrow streets of this rude, rough section of the city, back toward the temple.

Bad-Tibira was not a gentle place; Father's rule did not foster peace. I felt no fear, however, knowing if I were to reveal my face, no man would dare harm me. It was a hot night, and my melancholy was thick upon me, sorrow a dense knot in my heart, perhaps occluding my better judgement. I decided to pause at an inn for wine, against Irkalla's wishes.

The inn was a human establishment, and as a Nephilim, even in a commoner's robe, I stood out. Stares met me as I we entered, eyes following me, conversations halting momentarily.

"We should not be here, mistress," Irkalla whispered. "It is not safe."

I shushed her. "A cup of wine or two cannot do harm, Irkalla," I said. "And besides, what can a handful of drunk humans do to us? If they laid so much as a finger on me, they would find death close behind."

Irkalla sighed. "Still, Highness, it is not wise."

"A cup of wine, and then we go."

Irkalla nodded and waved the innkeeper over.

We took a bench in a dark corner of the inn, my hood pulled down despite the heat of the night and the oppressive humidity. I had a cup of wine in my hand, a rough carven vessel, faded and splintered, and the wine was bitter and heavily watered. Men filled the tavern, mostly *dumu-nita*—the unmarried freemen. They were young and rough looking, and they eyed me, obviously a woman alone with a single maidservant. They tried to get a glimpse under my hood, and a few even sauntered over and tried to talk to me. A glimpse of my glittering, golden Nephilim eyes sent them scurrying away easily enough; these human men had easier targets to woo than a Nephilim woman.

There was a table directly opposite mine, no more than four or five cubits away, and at it was a human male, sitting facing me. He too sat alone, swilling beer and digging idly at the scarred wood of the table with a fingernail. He was handsome, especially for a human. Even among Nephilim he would have been worth a second look, with striking blue eyes set in his thin, dark face, his sharp features framed by curly raven-black hair. Those ringlets drifted in front of his face from time to time, and he brushed them aside with a large hand calloused from work.

Oh, Inanna, he was handsome. Until I saw him, human men were all the same to me: small, weak, insignificant . . . but Japheth was different. No taller than most humans, he would be at least a foot shorter than me, and smaller all around, but his presence, his searing beauty, the intensity of his mere existence, made him seem every bit as huge and dominant as my many elder brothers. He wore a sleeveless tunic with a wide black leather belt and thick-soled sandals that strapped his calves up to his knees. His thick, muscular arms were bare in the flickering rush-light, and I found myself trying not to stare at him and failing . . . and wondering if perhaps a distraction was what I needed.

I rose unsteadily to my feet, ignoring Irkalla's hissed warnings and entreaties to come back, and skirted around my table. I accentuated the sway of my hips, pushing my hood back so that he might see me better as I approached his table. He looked at my face and at my hair in its intricate braids. His eyes took in my ears adorned with the finest jewels, my luminous golden eyes lined with kohl. He saw me, the handsome stranger, and he sat a bit straighter on the bench.

"May I join you?" I spoke in a low and sultry tone.

"Of course." His voice was smooth and deep, as he lifted his hand for the innkeeper.

He did not smile at me, but his gaze was fierce and unwavering.

The innkeeper brought a flagon of wine, and the beautiful human let his fingers brush mine as he poured the dark red liquid into my cup. A drop splashed onto my hand; I lifted my hand to my mouth and licked it away, slowly—this was no weak, watery wine poured for a wayward Nephilim woman intruding in a particularly-human place, no, this was fine, expensive wine, undiluted and potent.

He wore a strip of braided leather around his neck, hung with a copper pendant on which was inscribed a rune depicting the name of a human god, Elohim. Oh, that was brave, that was. My father's hatred for the many names of Elohim was widely known throughout Bad-Tibira and the surrounding lands. To openly show one's allegiance to The One God was tantamount to jumping into the Tiber at full flood. I grew up listening to the screams of prisoners who worshipped The One God, grew up watching my father cut off noses, strip away skin, and burn the soles of feet with red-hot sword tips.

Normally, I would have advised him to jump from the walls if he wished so much to die. As it was, I found his brash arrogance attractive, because anyone who would risk the wrath of my father for his God was a brave man indeed. My people were not brave, only foolish and arrogant and ignorant— their faith was no faith at all, only futile propitiation to empty gods, pointless offerings to blood-thirsty deities in hopes for a successful battle and more wealth.

I have observed those who worshipped the One God, and I have found their faith to be superior. They were willing, many of them, to die for their God, while my people would have denied their own fathers if it benefited them. These human Elohim-worshippers did not merely burn offerings, did not mutter a prayer to a statue and go about their way . . . no, they truly *believed*. The only question I had was whether the god they believed in so fiercely was any kinder than my gods . . . or any more real.

So here was this handsome human flaunting a name of the One God in an inn only a short walk from the palace . . . and I wanted him. I tried to blame it on the wine, but I cannot honestly say that drunkenness was the only reason for my desire. I might be unmarried, but I am no quivering virgin. I knew what I wanted: to feel his arms around me, to feel his hard chest beneath my hands. I wished to hear his voice, to know his name. Surely he was a lord, a great man, or a king from some foreign land. To be honest, however, I didn't care if he was an *arad*, a slave. I would have him. I vowed to Inanna that I would have him. After all, was I not the daughter of King Emmen-Utu, the greatest king of all the Nephilim?

He shifted in his seat and breathed deeply, peering at me, trying to discern my features in the gloom of the tavern.

"What is so lovely lady as you doing in so ugly a place as this?" He tried to sound casual, as if it were of minor interest to him.

The way he ran his tongue over his lips and dug his square-cut thumbnail into the tabletop belied his relaxed tone, and I unclasped the front of my cloak, let him see a bit of skin above the bodice of my dress.

"Does it matter?" I sipped my wine and let my interest burn in my eyes.

"No, Highness."

"Highness? What makes you think I am royalty? Perhaps I am just a servant girl wasting her mistress's time?"

"Ha!" His blue eyes flashed and he drank deeply of his wine. "And perhaps I am a priest of Enlil. Or wait, no, perhaps I am one of your father's guards, come to find you."

"You know who I am?"

"There is not another woman in all of Bad-Tibira half so beautiful as you, Princess Aresia. I know, for I have bedded many of them."

"An ugly ox-herder like you? I think not."

He leaned forward and said, "You don't think I'm ugly, Princess." He sounded confident of himself.

"Don't use my name so loudly," I murmured, and took a long drink of the wine. "And what makes you think so?"

"I saw the way you looked at me." He grinned, a flash of white teeth in the gloom. "It wasn't that difficult to interpret."

"How did I look at you, then?"

Damn him for being right; I buried my irritation in another swig of wine.

"Like a dog eying a scrap of meat." He smirked at me. "Hungrily."

"I did *not* look at you in any such fashion," I said, lifting my chin. "I am a princess and a Nephilim. I do not look at pathetic, lecherous humans with anything like *hunger*." I said this with more force than I had intended.

The wine and my lonely, bitter mood were beginning to win out over my self-control. I think this blue-eyed stranger knew this and was toying with me. I do not like being toyed with. Not one bit.

"You did, though, princess." He was mocking me . . . not laughing outright, but the corners of his mouth were tipped up slightly, and his eyes flashed with humor. "Exactly like a hungry dog. Not that I'm comparing you to a dog, mind you."

"I could have you killed for that, you know." I was definitely drunk now. "And don't call me princess."

I thought about trying to stand up and walk back to the palace, but judging by the way the table was dipping and swaying, I decided I had best stay put. And no more wine.

"You could," he was saying, "but you won't."

"How do you know?"

"One, because you're drunk." He ticked the numbers on his fingers as he spoke, "Two, even if you did call for the guards, they don't come here. Not at this time of night. And three, you're drunk—you need me to get you home. Do you see what I'm saying?" He was teasing, but also serious.

"I am . . . not . . . drunk." I think I was trying to convince myself, at that point, because I certainly wasn't convincing him. "And besides, I have my servant."

He just nodded and laughed, tossed back the dregs of his wine. "Listen—why don't you let me walk you home?" He was suddenly serious, glancing around at the other patrons of the tavern. "Both of you."

I followed his gaze and noticed, for the first time, everyone was watching us. There were more than a few angry faces, many hard pairs of eyes glaring at me. The room continued to spin, but the heady pleasantness had gone, leaving me dizzy and more than slightly panicked. Some of the eyes were, as this man had put it, eyeing me with . . . interest. They may not have known who I was, but if they did, they were unafraid. The only option I had, it seemed, was to let him walk me home. If anyone saw me and reported my presence outside the palace, Father would be furious with me; if anyone saw him, and more specifically, the pendant around his neck, he would be dragged to my father and tortured to death. But if I tried walking home alone, I was sure I would never make it. Not intact, anyway.

He stood up, held a hand out to me. "Are you coming, Lady?" The callouses on his palms scratched my fingers, his hand warm and strong.

He easily pulled me to my feet, despite our height difference, wrapping his arm around my shoulders and guiding me out the door. I felt many pairs of eyes watch me leave, heard a few feet scuff the packed dirt floor, benches scrape and cups clatter on tables. The arm around my shoulders hustled me out into the street, hesitated, and then pulled me away from the inn and back toward the palace. At least, I hoped he was taking me there. It occurred to me then, with his arm locked around me, that perhaps I had only gotten myself in a different kind of trouble. How did I know I could trust him? The fear bubbled up slowly, penetrating the haze of wine fogging my mind.

"Wait." I pulled him to a stop and wiggled out of his grasp. "How do I know you are not going to do the same thing to me?" It was hard to get the words out properly . . . I was a bit more drunk than I'd thought, it appeared.

He just chuckled and pulled me back into a fast, stumbling walk. "A bit late to think of that, Highness. You'll just have to trust me."

Irkalla was beside me, then, her arm in mine. "This is foolishness, mistress," she hissed. "He is a *human*."

If he had known me better, he would have known how impossible such a thing was for me. I did not trust *anyone*. My own father taught me this lesson. Among the Nephilim, we might sacrifice in the names of many gods, but our only real god was one's own self. My people would do and say anything to benefit themselves, and they would not spare a thought about how it affects anyone else. To trust another person is to invite trouble, and I had invited plenty for myself.

It was then I realized I had no idea where I was or where the palace was. And even if I had known, I was far too inebriated to be able to walk on my own. I was truly at the mercy of . . .

What was his name? Had I asked?

Ignoring Irkalla's words of caution I asked, "What is your name?" My words were slurred.

"Inanna help me," Irkalla murmured, irritation in her voice.

I ignored her and focused on the handsome human.

Embarrassment flushed through me, and I promised myself that I would never drink so much again. Not being in control of myself, of my words, of my fate, was enough to make me angry at myself. If I had been able to know, then, how fiercely my head would throb the next morning, I would have made a vow to Inanna herself, rather than just a promise in my own head.

"Finally she asks," he laughed. "I was wondering

if perhaps you had some secret Nephilim magic that allowed you to divine a man's name without asking. My name is Japheth, son of Noah."

"Japheth," I repeated, testing the flavor of his name on my tongue.

Japheth suddenly whirled around, shoving me against the wall with one hand and drew his *sappara*, a bronze sickle-sword, with his other. It happened so fast I never heard the attackers approach.

I had seen those weapons used before. The sappara had a crescent-shaped blade and a long handle wrapped in leather, with only the outside edge of the curve sharpened, the dull inner edge used as a hook to pull away shields or disarm an enemy. It was a difficult weapon to wield with any skill, but devastatingly effective when used by a master.

I was a woman and had never been to battle, but with five warrior brothers I'd learned my fair share about combat, so I knew a warrior when I saw one. Japheth was a dancing blur; each strike was done with a graceful, deadly economy that showed he was no stranger to battle. There were four of them, all humans, all burly, ugly, sweating, and porcine, all examples of the kind of humanity that made me understand—if not agree with—my father's animosity toward the race.

They were armed with short spears and battle-axes; they knew what they were doing . . .

And they wanted me and Irkalla both.

Three of them encircled Japheth, attacked him at once with a furious onslaught of blows; the fourth came at me, sword held low, left hand free and reaching for me, pink tongue licking his thick lips, as if already tasting my flesh. He expected me to be like his usual prey, soft, weak human girls incapable of defending themselves.

I was a Nephilim, and we were a race of warriors, even the women.

I used the razor edge of the obsidian dagger I kept hidden in my sleeve to split his belly like a sack of grain, spilling his intestines into the street. I cursed him, knocked him to his knees with the hilt of my dagger, and spat in his face. He was a fool if he thought a Nephilim princess would be easy prey. He came at me, thinking he could wave his sword and frighten me into spreading my knees for him.

Bah. Fool.

More fools they for assuming Japheth would be easy prey. An understandable mistake for he was not a large man, nor a lumbering brute like his attackers, but lithe and quick, striking serpent-fast, each motion flowing like water into the next. He used the hook-side of his sappara to turn aside a spear-thrust, twisting the handle with a flick of his wrist and the spear fell from his enemy's hand. Japheth grabbed the spear with his free hand, up high near the leaf-shaped blade, and thrust it into the man's belly and twisted it, wrenching a howl of agony from him. While he speared the man, his sword was not idle. He turned aside an axe and hacked into an exposed neck, dropping the second. The third realized he was outmatched and tried to run. His eyes were on Japheth, so he did not see me coming from the shadows to bury my blade in his throat. I was sprayed with his blood as he fell.

"My lady?" Japheth was next to me, wiping at my face with the edge of his robe. "Are you hurt?"

"No . . . no. The blood is theirs," I gestured to the bodies bleeding out into the sand. My hand was coated with in blood. "These aren't the first men you've killed."

"No, Highness. I served in your father's army. He may hate my people, but he'll conscript us to fight his wars readily enough." His voice was edged with bitterness.

Japheth hung the sappara from his belt, took my wrist, and cleaned my hand with his tunic. His fingers were warm on my skin; his touch sent a tingle up my arm.

"That is true enough. He puts your kind at the front and watches them die. He says they fall like heads of wheat under the sickle."

"Most do."

"But not you?" The adrenaline had washed away

the effects of the wine for the most part.

He let go of my hand and set off toward the palace. I took stride next to him, slipping my fingers in his. I felt bold, reckless; something about this man erased my prudence.

Following behind, Irkalla had given up trying to admonish me. I knew all she wanted now was to see me home, safely in my bed.

He looked down at our twined hands and then up at me, but he did not remove his hand from mine. "I am not like most men. Men, such as those back there, they would go down in battle like heads of wheat, as you have said. And even you Nephilim are not so hard to kill, if you're fast enough." He glanced sideways at me to assess the impact of his words.

"Do not let my brothers hear you say that," I said. "They will show you otherwise."

I hated my brothers. They were the worst examples of Nephilim manhood, brutal and arrogant beasts who delighted in the misfortune of others, with the lone exception, perhaps, of my eldest brother, Kichu. I hated them, but I respected them as warriors. I often watched them fight outside the walls when armies from neighboring cities came against us. Each one of them could hew down entire phalanxes of human men, swinging their massive spears in wide swaths, crushing heads and wrecking ribs, smashing with their bronze shields and stomping with their hobnailed sandals.

Japheth's eyes went dark and inscrutable at the mention of my brothers. "Your brothers are excellent warriors. I fought next to Kichu and Dummuzi when King Sin-Iddim brought his army from Larsa against us. On the battlefield they fight like demons from the underworld."

To the right of us, the main temple loomed black in the moonlight; ziggurat steps rose like stairs mounting to the heavens, torches flickering in evenly spaced sconces lining the ascent to the apex of the temple. Before us, the palace walls rose up, man-tall blocks of stone stacked high and thick to keep the masses out, guards patrolling on top of the walls. We ascended the steeply sloping hill, not hurrying but strolling slowly in the silver moonlight.

I liked the feel of Japheth's hand in mine, and wondered what it would be like to lie with him.

I had never been with a human, but many of my other handmaidens had, and I often listened to the stories they told while attending to me. I had a vision of him above me, dark hard arms beside my face, blue eyes locked on mine as we writhed together . . . I flushed at the thought, my heart beating like a fleeing hare.

I was more sober now, and the reckless determination to have him was not fading. If anything it was increasing, but sobriety brought with it a dose of reality. I still wanted him, but the consequences of doing so were bubbling up in my mind, growing stronger as we neared the palace. No, I told myself. Father would be outraged if he found me with a human, or even if he heard a rumor of it; I shuddered at the thought of what he would do Japheth.

My companion felt the shudder. "What is it, Highness?"

I couldn't tell him my thoughts. "Nothing, it is nothing. You had better let us walk alone from here. If the gate guards see you with me, it would cause problems for both of us. Especially if they were to recognize that rune you wear."

Japheth touched a finger to his pendant, as if remembering it was there. "Oh, this? I forget that I wear it, much of the time. It was a gift from my mother." He tucked it underneath the collar of his tunic.

"Is she dead, your mother?"

"No, but I haven't seen her in many years, mainly because my relationship with my father is . . . difficult. We may believe in the same God, but we do not believe in the same way. He is a hard man, my father."

That piqued my curiosity. "I would think he would be kind, being a follower of Elohim."

"He would be kind to you," Japheth said, his

voice bitter. "He spends hours talking of his God, and he would try to persuade you away from the false gods. But to me, his son, he is . . . demanding. He expects me to be as devoted as he is. 'Elohim demands our sacrifice,' he would say to me, even as a child. Sacrifice always meant work in the fields rather than playing with my brothers. Sacrifice meant doing as Father demanded. His devotion to God takes precedence over everything, including his family." He sighed and shook his head. "But that was a long time ago, and I'm sure you don't want to hear about that."

"Oh, you might be surprised what I would be interested in." I let my voice communicate what I could not say out loud.

It might be a risk, but I wanted this man. There was a battle raging inside me, and my prudence was burned away by the fire of his touch, the lightning in his gaze. Japheth heard it and pulled me to a stop, pressing my back against the cold stone of the palace wall. His eyes met mine, his hands resting on my waist, and he kissed me. I felt his heart beating against my breast, hard and fast, thumping like the drums of war. His kiss was tender, despite the fierce throb of his heart. I felt myself floating away, felt my hands on his muscular chest and face, felt his hands wandering from my waist downward to caress my backside, and I felt my body responding to his touch. For a delicate, wondrous moment, all I knew was his lips and our exploring hands.

A footstep scuffed in the dirt nearby, and for a moment I saw my father's wide, scarred face in my mind, golden eyes sparking with fury. I pulled away, trembling slightly—it was only a temple prostitute scurrying back to the temple, but the moment of passion was gone.

I shook my head, "We cannot do this. My father will kill you, and he will torture you for days you before he lets you die."

"I am not afraid of your father," he said, leaning in again.

I pulled away, but let my hands stay on his chest. I did not want to pull away, I wanted to kiss him again, but fear of my father won out. "You *should* be. If you think my brothers are demons, then my father is Ninurta himself. He is *evil*, Japheth. He delights in causing pain to followers of Elohim . . . and I am his only daughter."

He was insistent, smiling his contempt. "I don't care. We're out here and he's in there somewhere," he nodded at the palace, toying with a lock of my hair. "I'm not going to let you kiss me like that and then run off and hide behind your father."

This brought a flush of anger in me. "*You* kissed *me*! And I'm not hiding behind my father. I'm trying to protect you, you fool."

"I don't need protecting." Anger flashed in his eyes despite his calm tone. His fingers tightened on my arms.

This had all happened so fast. I still felt the tingle of his lips on mine, and the thrill of his hands on my waist just above the swelling curve of my buttocks. His skin was warm and I wanted to kiss him again. I wanted to sneak him into the palace and bring him to my chambers and love him there beyond moonrise and into the dawn.

Instead, I jerked myself out of his arms and fled, Irkalla right behind me.

# CHAPTER 2

## The Wickedness of Man

"The Lord saw that the wickedness of man
was great in the earth, and that every intention
of the thought of his heart was only evil
continually." Genesis 6:5 (ESV)

O H, INANNA. I COULD NOT GET HIM OUT OF MY
head. I had heard the maidservants speak
of being lovestruck and heartsick and had always
mocked them for it. Foolishness, I would say,
mooning over block-headed men. But now I was
caught up in this web, and I could not extract myself
from it. I knew, too, that it would be my downfall.

I saw it in visions, feared it in the deepest places
of my soul, but I could not deny the events that came
upon me, one after the other like stones tumbling
down a hill before an avalanche. It was foolishness,

and I knew it well. He was a human, and a common-er. I was Nephilim, and a princess. It was my destiny to be married to a king and bear royal children, to keep my race alive and strengthen the kingdom. A human man had no part in that. All I would accomplish would be to get him tortured and killed, and bring trouble down upon my own head.

*I will simply stay in the palace*, I told myself.

*I will be safe in here, and he will be safe out there.*

We would each be safer apart. I would forget him.

But I was weak. Or perhaps my destiny was not so indelibly written as I had thought. I'd stopped believing in the gods of my father and my people a very long time ago. I think I first realized our gods were empty and lifeless statues when I watched my mother die.

I offered burnt offerings to the gods, begging them to give her back to me. I prayed to the gods, I brought grain and fatted calves and gold and jewels, and I wept before their altars, and yet always were they silent. I sat beside my mother when she lay still and pale on her deathbed, her once beautiful and now-frail body swathed in fine linens and glistening with the ointments and unguents of the priests and healers. I sat beside her corpse, praying. There were no last words, no weak squeeze of my hand. Just a hollow aching silence.

My girlhood died with her; my faith in Anu and Enlil and Ereshkigal and Inanna died with her; my capacity for love died with her.

Or so I thought, until I felt Japheth's lips upon me, felt his eyes devouring my body as I ran away from him. I knew him not at all, had no understanding of his character. But yet, I did. I *knew* him, I felt his very soul brush up against mine as we kissed, and felt its touch as a familiar caress. I thought I loved him, as foolish as it was. The moment I kissed him, I felt as if I loved him, and knew even then that it was foolish and dangerous.

That very night as I ran to the gate, Irkalla slipping another coin into the guards' hands to buy their silence, as we ghosted through the deserted palace hallways to my private chambers . . . that very night I knew I loved him. I knew also that I should not. But yet I did, and I could no more escape it than I could bring my mother back to life.

I crept into my bed, and moments later I heard Irkalla, my handmaiden, come into my chamber. She perched on the edge of my bed and unbraided my hair. I refused to speak first, knowing would she would not approve of my actions with the human Japheth, and I did not wish to hear her lectures.

Perhaps she could convince me to abandon my folly; Inanna knew I could not convince myself.

All I knew were his lightning-blue eyes, the deadly grace of his movements, and the tender touch of his lips, the inciting blaze of his hands on my body.

Oh gods, I was in trouble.

"Mistress," Irkalla said, eventually, "we are more than princess and servant, I should like to think. Please, if you harbor any affection for me at all, please . . . do not have anything more to do with that human."

"His name is Japheth, son of Noah. He is a warrior, and he believes in The One God." The last few words were whispered, even in the privacy of my own bedchamber.

"A worshipper of Elohim? You know better, mistress." Her voice dropped to a whisper so quiet I barely heard her. "If your father even hears a *rumor* of you being seen with a human, much less a believer in *that* god—he would raze the entire city looking for him, and he would turn you out into the wilderness to be eaten by lions."

I sighed. "Irkalla, why does he hate them so much? I've long wondered, and I can't figure it out. I know what happened with my mother made things worse, but that doesn't explain it . . . not entirely."

Irkalla's hands, gently untangling the snarls in my hair, stilled and rested on my shoulders. "I do not know all the details, because what little I know myself is from rumors and stories whispered amongst the older servants. I have heard that your father once loved a human woman by the name of Lily. He would have been very young indeed when all this occurred. He was rebellious in his youth, they say, refusing to take up his responsibilities as the crown prince, preferring instead to dice with the soldiers, and spend his time drinking and gambling and whoring.

"Well, they say that he met a beautiful human woman, and they fell in love. All the human women loved him, back then, despite his reputation. He cut quite a figure, I would imagine, for he is still an attractive man, even in his age. Well, one day, he and his human lover were out in the forest, lying together in the grass, naked and spent after—"

"Irkalla! I do *not* wish to hear that about my own father!"

"Forgive me, mistress, I am but telling the story as I have heard it told. Anyway, they were lying together in the forest, drowsing and talking sleepily, as couples do in such moments, when they heard twigs snapping and the sounds of branches scraping against metal.

"They sat up and found themselves surrounded by men—humans—dozens of them, armed with spears and shields and daggers and axes. The human men were jealous, you see, especially one in particular, who also loved Lily. Emmen—for he was not king then and had not yet earned the favor of Utu the sun god—Emmem had stolen all of their finest women and soiled them with his rapacious appetite. They flocked to him, and he bedded them all, willing or no.

"They greatly underestimated him. He snatched up his spear and set among them, still naked, killing many of them. In the end, they managed to wound him, fatally, or so they thought. Near dead and mad with rage, Emmen could only watch as the human men took their turns upon poor Lily, and when they had finished with her, they slew her, Emmen watching helplessly all the while.

"He healed quickly, as our people do, and when he had regained his strength, he took his revenge. He found those men, each and every one of them, and he killed them all, brutally, savagely. But he wasn't satisfied with merely slaying them. Oh no, not Emmen, as you might well imagine. He ripped them asunder, they say, tore them limb from limb with his bare hands and scattered the bloody pieces throughout the city, and ever since then, your father has borne an unreasoning hatred of humans. Although, knowing what those men did, I do not blame him for hating them."

I was silent, thinking. I had never heard this story before, but it made sense to me. I wished I could ask him about it, but something told me that he would only fly into a rage if I brought it up.

"I wish I could say I did not believe it," I said, finally, "but I know my father all too well. He is absolutely capable of something like that, and it would explain his animosity toward humans."

"It is a story I have heard more than once," Irkalla said, "from many sources, and the details have changed very little in the telling. The lesson you should glean from this story, mistress, is that if your father discovered you consorting with a human male, it would enrage him, and I do not wish to consider what he would do . . . either to you or to your human."

"I *know*, Irkalla. I know. I have had the same thought, believe me." I ducked my head, and mumbled the next words. "I . . . I love him."

"You *love* him?" The scornful sarcasm of her words angered me, but I kept silent and waited for the rest. "How long have you known him, mistress? A matter of minutes? You know nothing about him whatsoever, and even less of love. You cannot *love* him, Aresia, if you do not *know* him. You may *want* him, and you may find him handsome. He may make your heart flutter and your body ache with lust for him, but *love*? I think not, lady."

I knew she was right, but the bright, brief, hot flare of infatuation was more intoxicating than any wine.

I truly did try to stay away. I stayed in the palace until I was crazy with boredom and mad with desire for Japheth. His face was ever in my mind; my skin remembered the tingle of his touch. I even went to the temple and offered sacrifices to the gods and prayed to them to remove the desire from me.

The gods were silent, as they ever were.

I thought of praying to Elohim, but I did not know how; I knew prayer to The One God was not like prayer to my people's gods. Would He listen to my prayers? Me, a Nephilim, whose father persecuted His followers, tortured them with fire and knives, killed them with his bare hands? I thought not, and so kept my prayers to myself.

But I was weak, and I ended up in his arms before the week was out.

I snuck out of the palace, this time during the day and without Irkalla. I found him loitering outside the palace in the shadow of the ziggurat, sharpening the blade of his sappara absently, the whetstone sliding across the bronze with a rasping metallic ring.

"I thought you would never come," he said, rising to his feet as I approached, my hood drawn and my head ducked.

Before I had time to even respond, his hands were around my waist and his lips on mine, his hand on the back of my neck, drawing me down for a kiss. I tried, even then, to protest, but the words were lost before they were born.

I should have pulled away, should have run back home, but I didn't. I kissed him back, and lost myself in the flavor of his lips and the touch of his hands; so lost was I in his kiss that it was he who pulled away first.

"Come," he told me, pulling me by the hand. "We can't stay here. The guards will see us and the game will be up before it's begun."

I let him lead me through a maze of streets and tight alleys, ducking through the narrow spaces between houses, skirting humble temples to minor deities, slipping around clumps of people coming and going and loitering and begging and buying and selling. The scent of roasting meat and grilling vegetables and spices and unwashed bodies assaulted us at every turn. I followed him because I trusted him, which my mind told me was stupid, but upon which my heart was immoveable.

The hood of my cloak fell back as we hurried, revealing my face to the crowded street. I had come out at midday, because it was then that I could no longer hold myself back. I heard people muttering, "It's the princess, it's her . . ." and I knew we were in trouble. I felt eyes on me, hated the feel of them searching, examining, accusing, judging. Hand in hand with a human I fled through the streets, expecting at every turn to be stopped by palace guards. We weren't being pursued, or watched— that we were aware of—but I think we had a feeling, deep down and unnameable, that we should not be caught or seen, that we should not be together like this in broad daylight, with all the city watching. There was no law against humans and Nephilim being together . . . but me, the only daughter of King Emmen-Utu, and a follower of Elohim? Foolishness.

I ignored the cautioning of my head, giving over instead to the song of my body, the thunder of my pulse at the feel of his hand in mine, the burning tingle of my lips where he'd kissed me. I let him lead me, watching his back twist, his broad shoulders move. Watching his taut backside shift as he wove a path through the thronging market crowds. Merchants hawked their wares, calling out the prices for dates and figs and pistachios and grapes, gold rings and cheap baubles, hand woven rugs, spices . . . I heard the familiar cacophony of the market, felt the press of bodies around me, but had eyes only for Japheth.

Eventually, we left behind the bazaar at city-center, and I found myself in a part of the city to which I'd never ventured before: the tight, shadowy, twisting streets where houses were stacked two and three high, accessible only by narrow staircases that were more truly ladders than stairs. Here, the houses were built right up against the city wall itself, stacked like towers of blocks leaning against each other. If I were to stand in the window of a house on one side of the street, I could reach out my arm and touch the windowsill of the house opposite, so narrow were these streets, and yet now and again we had to press ourselves against the wall as flat as we could to make way for a wagon drawn by onagers—a race of donkeys native to this region, used widely among humans and Nephilim alike to draw carts and plow fields and carry burdens, since they are hardy, powerful, intelligent, and loyal, if a bit recalcitrant.

Japheth made his way unerringly through the maze to where the narrow alley-like streets intersected with the wide thoroughfare of the main road running straight as an arrow shaft from city gate to palace gate, the main road swept clean by the king's order and the gate within shouting distance of the houses against the wall. I was closer to this part of Bad-Tibira than I'd ever been without Father's troop of guards and the security of a slave-borne litter.

He led me to a stack of houses directly against the wall, close enough to the gate that I could hear the bawdy jokes of the guards as they idly scrutinized the foot traffic entering and exiting the city. Up, then, ascending one of those narrow ladder-like staircases to the second level. The home below smelled of animal fat being rendered into candle wax. Japheth's home was tiny, a single room barely wide enough for a pallet and a few baskets of belongings, the ceiling low enough that the top of my head brushed against it if I stood upright; this was a uniquely human dwelling, and not meant for the height of a Nephilim.

Here, in his home, I felt our differences keenly. As a Nephilim, I would be alive centuries after he was long in his grave. I stood several inches taller than he, and even as a woman possessed greater total strength. My eyes glowed golden, as all did those of every Nephilim, a gift from the gods who were our ancestors. He was a human, merely a human, and not even a king or a renowned warrior.

But yet, standing facing him, his eyes blue as the sky, hot as lightning bursting from thunderheads . . . I didn't care about any of that. Our differences faded to dust under the heat of his gaze.

"Princess—" he began.

"Aresia," I interrupted. "I do not always wish to be a princess. Certainly not now, and certainly not here."

He gestured at the pallet that was his bed, a thin

nest of threadbare blankets on the floor. "I have no fine linen sheets to offer, Aresia."

We were separated by a handful of feet, me on the far side of the room, he with his back to the door, the rude bed between us.

"I don't care," I said, and took a step closer to him.

He unbuckled the wide belt around his waist, tossed it aside, and hauled the garment off, standing before me in nothing but a thin cotton undergarment. "I have no money for gifts, either."

I tugged a thick, golden, ruby-encrusted cuff off my wrist and tossed it aside carelessly. "Gold and jewels I possess in abundance."

He took a step toward me, tugged the strap of my dress aside, so the garment sagged, displaying the upper portion of my breasts. "I am a human, the son of a poor farmer." The other strap followed suit, and then only the tips of my breasts held up my dress. "My family worships Elohim."

I stood still as a statue, barely breathing, as my dress drooped lower and lower. If I took a breath, if I filled my lungs and let my chest swell, the garment would fall . . . I wore no undergarments, so that single breath would leave me naked.

"I care for none of that," I whispered.

"Shouldn't you?" he asked, tracing a fingertip down between my breasts.

"Yes," I answered. "But I do not. Not now, anyway."

He hooked a fingertip inside the bodice, his blue eyes on mine. "And you want this?"

The stories my maids and servants had told me ran through my head, whispered tales of lying with mortal men, the thrill of it, the rush . . . how different human men were from Nephilim. I wanted this; I wanted *him*. My people placed no special significance upon virginity, and even marriage was only a tool for politics, except perhaps among commoners.

Thus, I was not a virgin, and this would not be my first time with a man, but it would be my first time with a human man, and I felt the excitement of it burning in my blood, as well as the forbidden nature of this meeting. If I were dawdling with a Nephilim guard, Father would not care. If I was running away with that guard, he would not care, although he would bring me back and remind me of my duty to the kingdom, my destiny to marry a king and rule as queen. But this? Sneaking across the city to dally with a *human*? This wasn't just taboo, this wasn't just foolish, this was . . . dangerous. And that was part of the excitement.

"Aresia, I need an answer." He traced the line of my breastbone from my throat to the swell of my cleavage.

In answer, I took a deep breath, allowing my

chest to expand, shifting off the tenuous purchase of the dress on my breasts. The expensive purple linen slid down, billowed off me and pooled on the floor, leaving me naked in front of Japheth. He sucked in a breath, his gaze raking over me appreciatively.

*Touch me*, I thought, willing him to hear what I was not speaking.

He touched a palm to my waist, his hand hard and callused and warm on my flesh. I held my breath, then, as his touched drifted to my backside, he pulled me against him. I felt all of him, and desire boiled inside me. I pushed his undergarment off and grasped him. I lowered my face to his and claimed a kiss, and, after a delirious moment, Japheth took that kiss and made it his, took control of it, guiding me to the pallet of blankets and laid me on them, hovering over me.

This was the vision I'd first had of him, when I first met him: his arms beside my face, his hair tangled and curly and drifting over his vivid blue eyes. This was real, though, his body warm and hard and heavy on mine as he devoured me with his mouth, his hands. I returned the fervor, seeking his flesh, clasping and caressing his muscles, digging my fingers into his skin, nipping at his lips. He nestled against me, and I lifted my hips and gasped as we joined, and neither of us dared look away.

It was everything my servants had claimed it

would be, and more. Or perhaps it was just Japheth, his intensity, and his fire.

We moved together with the midday sun streaming through his window, the shouts of guards and merchants outside the window, and my cries of pleasure were lost in the noise of the city and the bustle of the crowds at the gate.

Every day I snuck out of the palace, Irkalla hiding my absences with excuses and pleas of ignorance— she's on her courses and won't leave her rooms; she's been sick and is still recovering; she does not tell me everywhere she goes, for I am but a humble slave . . .

If anyone was suspicious, no one said anything to me. Irkalla was disapproving, but more out of fear than true disapproval. If my other servants knew, they said nothing—they knew I'd reassign them to one of my brother's wives if they did, and those women were far less benevolent than I.

It began innocuously, as such things do: passionate pleasure, the rush of excitement, the thrill of the danger. But it gradually became something else. As one day became another, and then one week became two, my desire for Japheth's body became a desire for more of him. A need to be near him. We spoke little enough, preferring to do our communication with our bodies rather than our words, but when we did speak, it was always easy to talk to him. The stories we told were idle banter, the kind of light, easy things couples whisper of in the glowing moments after pleasure is spent.

He told stories of his battles, and I told stories of the court, and we never spoke of what we were doing, or of deeper things, such as our emotions. And we never spoke of the danger we faced if we were ever caught.

In truth, I think we both knew it was always destined to end, that our days together were numbered, and thus we never spoke of the future. Except for that one time when we first met, he never spoke of his family, nor did I.

He was gone for a day or two or three now and then, and once for over a week—working as guard in a merchant's caravan, he told me. But as weeks turned into a month, I was still sneaking out at dawn or in the small hours of the night to see Japheth. I never stopped to wonder what would happen if I had gotten with child by Japheth, though it was not common for a human male to impregnant a female Nephilim—not impossible, only unlikely.

Irkalla became ever more restless, began entreating me to stay in the palace more often. The servants began to whisper when they thought I wasn't looking, and the guards began watching me come and go. They always saw, but I always thought of guards as just part of the palace, as much as if they were doors or vases or tapestries or servants.

Irkalla, however . . . her worry turned to fear, and her pleas began to filter through to my better sense.

"You will be caught," she would plead with me when I returned to my rooms, drifting easily on feet still light from recent pleasure, my skin still flushed. "You will be caught, and it go hard for you and worse for him."

She pleaded with me to end my dalliance with Japheth, to find a Nephilim man to distract myself with, or devote myself to Inanna—anything but continue my secret affair with Japheth.

I knew the dangers, but I didn't think them worth considering. Not when there was such delirious pleasure in Japheth's arms.

I made light of her pleas, and when that did not work, I ignored her.

But, of course, Irkalla's fears were realized.

It was the month of Arah Tisritum, two months after I met him, two months of days and nights spent losing myself in Japheth. Two months of discovering the deepest pleasures of the flesh.

It was just past sunset, the evening sky red as blood. If I had bothered to look, it was an omen I should have seen.

Japheth and I had met at the bazaar, as we always did, and were walking to his house by the wall, taking a circuitous route, keeping to side streets, my hood drawn. We rounded a corner, and Japheth skidded to a sudden stop, and I slammed into him from behind. There, standing before us, his eight-foot-tall frame slouched easily against a wall, his burly arms crossed, his face clouded with puzzled anger, was my oldest brother, Kichu. His broad, scarred face and golden eyes seared into me, disapproving.

"What are you doing, Aresia?" he demanded. He reached for me with a calloused paw; I pulled out of reach. "You shouldn't be here. You belong in the palace. And what are you doing with *Japheth*?" He obviously knew Japheth personally, but kept his focus on me.

"I can do what I want, Kichu. I'm not a child." I cursed silently, because I had sounded exactly like a child.

"You're coming with me, Aresia. Father will not be pleased with you."

"I will not!"

Kichu looked from me to Japheth. "Don't be a fool, Japheth. You know what you risk. If I respect any human, it's you, but I cannot help you if you continue in this."

Kichu was the least vile, the least despicable of

my brothers, so if I could worm my way out this with anyone, it would be him.

"I'm not doing anything wrong, Kichu," I said, in my most convincing voice. "Just pretend you didn't see anything. Please?"

My brother sighed and scratched his beard.

"Fine," he growled. "But only this once. And no more of this. You, Aresia—you will stay in the palace. And you, Japheth, will stay away from my sister. She is not for you." He turned on his heel and stalked off.

I looked to Japheth, expecting to see resignation on his face.

"What?" He pulled me up against him, smirking arrogantly. "Do you think I am so easily dissuaded? I told you, your brothers don't scare me. I know what I want, and I will not be frightened away like some puling servant boy." He stopped suddenly and leveled an intent, searching gaze at me. "Unless you would rather return to the palace? I will take you back, if you wish . . ."

He was teasing me. Damn him, he knew he could goad me, prod me, manipulate me. I glared at him, but he just grinned and resumed walking.

"I didn't think so." A tease, those words.

"You are arrogant," I said, each word crisp and clear. My attempt to get the upper hand only seemed to amuse him further.

"Yes, I am. And you love it."

He kissed me hard and deep, right there in the street, and pinched my backside hard enough to elicit a surprised squeal. I cursed him, slapped him. My hand cracked loudly against his face, leaving a red handprint, drawing gazes and a few chuckles from passersby.

He just laughed and rubbed his face. "Temper, temper, princess. You'll draw attention, acting like that."

He drew me into a walk, then, and we went to his house and divested each other of our garments and lost ourselves in the now familiar dance of flesh on flesh.

I thought the matter of my brother was ended.

It wasn't that day, nor the next, but nearly a full week later. Dawn, the sky just beginning to lighten from black to gray, the air sharp with cold, our breath frosting in the air as we wound our way from his house back to the palace.

Less than fifty yards from the side gate through which I normally entered, we were confronted by a phalanx of Nephilim warriors. The captain stepped forward, a small, barrel-chested man with an oily, curled beard and a scar running from left eye to right mouth corner.

"Japheth, son of Noah, son of Lamech, son of Methuselah. You will come with us." He pounded his spear-butt into the ground, and the phalanx split apart and surrounded us in a neat, precise maneuver.

I recognized the captain: he was my father's personal bodyguard, and procurer—a title Father had given him; a grand sounding title, to be sure, but all it meant was Enkidu had the authority to snatch anyone off the streets and drag him before Father for "questioning," meaning torture. Enkidu was a vicious, bloodthirsty monster who delighted in the shrill sound of screams and the salty tang of spilled blood. That he was here meant that Japheth had been identified to Father as a worshipper of Elohim. He hadn't looked at me, yet, so perhaps . . .

"And you, Princess Aresia." He grabbed me by the wrist before I could even blink, a motion faster than I would have thought possible. "You, girl, are in trouble. Half the city has seen you with this *human* . . . this God-worshipper. Your father is ready to rip the city into broken bits, Highness."

Out of the corner of my eye I saw Japheth fingering his sappara. I still had my left hand on his bicep, and I squeezed it, tried to beg him wordlessly not to throw his life away; even he couldn't best this many warriors. He flashed me a fierce grin belied by the glittering hatred in his eyes. Lightning struck then, a bronze gleam in the early morning haze. The sappara buried itself in Enkidu's neck, nearly severing it, and the hand on my wrist fell away. What a fool—brave and deadly, but a fool. This thing between us was not worth him dying.

Before the rest of the soldiers could close in, I threw myself in front of Japheth, facing him. "Please, Japheth, don't do this! I can reason with Father, perhaps get you freed. Don't throw your life away. Not like this."

The soldiers hesitated, knowing their orders were to bring both of us alive. Father liked to torture his victims himself, so he would not be best pleased if Japheth was brought to him already dead. But Enkidu was lying slain in the sand, and they couldn't let that go unrequited.

"Move out of the way, Princess," one of them said, gesturing with his spear. "Move aside, before you get hurt."

Japheth stared into my eyes, and I saw desperation in his gaze, something that went deeper. "I won't be tortured, Aresia . . . not again." Fear lived there, deep in his soul.

I wondered what he meant . . . *not again*?

I squeezed his hands in mine. "I won't let that happen. Just go with them."

"You can't stop your father. You know it as well as I."

"Japheth . . ." I was selfish; I could not watch him die. I should have moved out of the way, let my father's men hack him to pieces, but I simply could not. "Please. *Please.*"

He breathed in deeply, steeling himself, and dropped his sappara to the dirt. He moved away from me, and I could see panic warring with determination in his face, and I knew then that whatever we had was more than mere stolen moments of pleasure.

The soldiers stepped forward, grabbed him, and dragged him away. One of them turned back to make sure I was watching, then raised the hilt of his short sword and smashed Japheth on the skull, loosing a ribbon of blood, and my handsome, blue-eyed human slumped in his captor's arms, unconscious.

The last I saw of Japtheth was his feet trailing in the sand, his Nephilim captors towering over him.

The desperation I felt then went deeper than I had ever expected; sometimes, I think, we do not truly understand the depth of our own feelings toward someone until that person is taken away from us. Now that he was gone, his death imminent, I fully realized he meant far more to me than merely a source of forbidden pleasure. If that was all this was, I should not have cared if Father got his hands on Japheth. I might have argued for his life, of course, but . . . this?

As Father's personal guards dragged Japheth's body away, I felt a hollow in the pit of my stomach, a panic in my heart, a blind, unreasoning fear in my brain.

I knew what Father was going to do to Japheth, and the thought had my heart sinking, had everything inside me rebelling.

I couldn't let that happen. Not to Japheth. He'd done nothing wrong but give me what I wanted; why should he die for that?

I sank back against the wall and prayed to Elohim, begging him to spare Japheth. I prayed to a god I didn't believe in, but who seemed in that moment more real than any of the gods of my own people.

I hadn't meant to pray at all, really, the words merely poured out of me, unbidden: "Spare him, Elohim. Spare him." The words were whispered aloud. "I do not worship you, because I do not know you. Perhaps you cannot hear my prayers because I am a Nephilim, but if you can, please . . . spare him. If you let him live, I swear to you I will worship you and you alone. Please."

I did not feel an answer, did not hear His Voice speaking to me. All I heard was the beating of my own heart, the scuffling feet of passers-by, the harsh cry of ravens and twittering of sparrows. Did He hear me, The One God? Do the prayers of one such as I matter to Him?

A hand grasped my arm and pulled me into a

walk. It was a soldier, barely more than a boy, his thin beard still scraggly and sprouting, his hand trembling. "You must come with me, Princess. Please."

Ha! A scared boy this was, afraid to lay hands on the princess. I snatched my arm from him, spat at his feet in contempt.

"Do not dare touch me, you filthy pig. I will walk alone." The boy just trembled harder, swallowed, and fell into step behind me.

My father was furious, of course; I had not expected anything else. The boy-soldier led me through the gate into the palace, and I looked up, as was my habit, at the heads impaled there. Gruesome reminders of my father's rage, those rotting skulls. Would Japheth's skull soon adorn the gate next to the thieves and worshippers of Elohim? Ravens and crows fluttered in perpetual flocks, fighting for morsels, cawing for eyeballs and batting at each other with wings for strips of flesh. I had a vision of Japheth, one blue eye lifeless and still vivid, the other pecked clean, flesh cut ragged at the neck and bones showing in patches on his skull. My stomach turned at the vision, and I had to breathe deeply and swallow quickly to douse the urge to vomit.

I could not, would not, let that happen.

"Damn you, daughter!" My father's voice rang out, the harsh boom echoing in the throne room, sending chills down my spine. "I've not asked much of you, Aresia. I did not marry you off when it would have benefited the kingdom. I have left you to your own devices, thinking you knew better than . . . than *this*." He was no longer yelling, but hissing, whispering, which sent needles of fear spiking through me more than any bellowing.

"I'm sorry, Father." *Short answers*, I reminded myself. *Don't argue with him.*

"Sorry is not *nearly* enough. Not only do I discover that you've been sneaking out of the palace and crawling around among those *vermin* . . . those *humans* . . . but you've been consorting with an Elohim worshipper? What else have you been doing? Prostituting yourself with the whores of Inanna perhaps?"

He was incoherent, spitting mockery of the very goddess to whom he sacrificed every feast-day. He paced from wall to wall, slamming the butt of his spear into the polished stone floor with cracks resounding like thunder. He stopped in front of me, broad chest heaving, and spittle at the corners of his mouth, his eyes narrowed and glaring and incandescent with rage, his fingers tightening on the haft of his spear. My father was a frightening figure

under the best of circumstances, standing six cubits tall—a full cubit taller than I, and close to three
cubits taller than the tallest human—his arms and
chest heavy with muscle even as his hair grayed
with age. His flesh bore a maze of scars, which told
the tale of many battles fought and won.

In his anger he was utterly terrifying—a god
made mad.

I wondered if maybe he truly was mad—perhaps the centuries of war had loosed his brain in his
skull . . . I did not know. I only knew I was more
afraid of him at that moment than ever before. He
looked perfectly capable of driving his fifteen-foot-
long spear into my belly and throwing me off the
balcony. Indeed, this was not fury; this was madness, pure and terrible. I tensed myself for a blow,
for the stab of spear-blade.

It never came.

He turned abruptly and strode back to his
throne, slumping down into the cushions and pillows. A goblet of wine was thrust tentatively into his
massive hand, and he quaffed deeply. He was making me wait; this was a favorite tactic of his—the
condemned would stand shaking in the coolness of
the throne room, listening to the King's breathing
and wine-gulps and belching, all the while wondering what their fate was to be.

"Bring him in," my father ordered.

I nearly fainted, for I knew what he planned. He would not punish me directly, but he would focus on Japheth instead. I wanted to weep at the thought, but I couldn't . . . wouldn't. I heard a door slam, then the scrape of dragging feet and the rattle of jangling chains. Two guards appeared from a side-entrance, Japheth between them. Blood streamed from his nose and mouth, his lips were puffed and split, his eyes bruised black. He was limp in the arms of his jailers. This was no act; Japheth was proud and would not feign weakness to glean sympathy.

I couldn't stop a tear from escaping, and I averted my eyes.

*Elohim, save him. Save him.* The prayer crossed my mind unbidden.

He was dumped at the bottom of the dais to lie motionless at my father's feet. The king rose and knelt near Japheth's head, grabbed a hank of hair and lifted him so Japheth's swollen eyes met his. "Japheth, son of Noah . . . did you think I would not find out? I would slit your throat here and now, but that would be too quick. Your pain will teach my foolish daughter a lesson."

Japheth cracked an eye open, regarded my father with a bleary-eyed gaze, head wobbling. He drew a breath, moaned, planted his palms on the floor and pushed himself up. My father backed off, amused, watching as Japheth struggled to his knees, attempting to rise, only to fall back to the floor. Hands flat against the stone again, his breathing labored, blood and drool pooling beneath his chin, Japheth rose to his knees again, and this time stayed there, facing the king, staring up defiantly at the giant towering over him.

"I curse you, Emmen, son of Dagon, son of Sargon." Japheth's voice was strong and unwavering, his words ringing clearly in the hall; he paused, wiped the blood from his face with a forearm. "You are a maggot before the will of The One God, and you will die like the insect you are, squirming in the mud. You will die, and all your might will not save you."

No one had ever, *ever* spoken to my father like that. There was an odd tone in Japheth's voice, a hollow, absent note that somehow seemed familiar.

It struck me in a flash: many years ago, when I was a girl still reeling from my mother's death, there was an ancient human beggar woman that loitered near the gate to the palace. Old and tottering and blind and frail. Her eyes were clouded gray, her skin hung in wrinkled bags from her bones, and her hair was little more than a few, thin, lank, yellow-white strings. Kichu often used to walk with me to the palace gate, and sometimes just beyond, and he would buy me trinkets from gold sellers and toys from traveling merchants.

He found the old beggar woman amusing, and would stop to converse with her. He would provoke her, I realized later, until she became irate and cast curses on him, calling down the wrath of her One God on him, prophesysing Kichu's doom. Usually he laughed at her and mocked her but never caused her harm and would always toss her a coin before he departed. Once, however, her words did not amuse him, and I think he always carried those words with him; I know I never forgot them.

She had begun with the usual curses, screaming insults and calling on Elohim to strike him dead. "Elohim will punish you," she wailed. "You will not escape his wrath! Turn away, mighty prince! Silence your mockery!"

Kichu had just chuckled at this and dug in a pouch for a coin. His hand was arrested midway, however, when her voice changed, and her blind eyes closed, her normally hunched back straightened and her head was thrown back, her mouth stretched wide in a rictus. Words had emitted from her, but they were not in her voice, and her lips had not moved as she spoke.

"Death will find you, Kichu, son of Emmen, son of Dagon," she had croaked, her voice low and echoing and guttural and not her own normal shrill shriek. "You will walk this earth for many years to come, and you will find victory among the fields of war. Your wives will bear you many sons and daughters, and you will rule over men. You will stride with arrogance, and life will taste as honey on your lips. But death will find you, and will replace the sweetness of life with bitter gall of tragedy. Death will roll down upon you; the skies will break open and rain horror upon you and upon your people. Your sons and your daughters and your wives will drown before your eyes, their heads will be broken upon the palace roof, and you will watch them die. Death will find you, and your mighty arms will not stay its touch. Call out to The One God for mercy, Kichu, son of Emmen, son of Dagon, for your death is certain."

Kichu had cursed in a whisper, striking the old woman with a fist and then dragging me back to the palace where he threw me into Irkalla's arms. When I had seen him next, his eyes were haunted, and I knew then that the woman's words had driven a dagger of doubt into his heart.

Japheth's words in that moment to my father sounded as that beggar woman's had, so many years earlier. They were not spoken in his voice, but in the voice of prophecy, the words croaked and guttural and hollow and echoing with deep, thrumming power.

My father was still for a fraught moment, and then he struck Japheth with the flat of his spear-blade, knocking him to the floor. "Your death will be slow," my father said, just loud enough for me to hear. "I will make your agony last for days. I will rip out your fingernails. I will tear out your tongue with my bare hands. I will rip the skin from your bones and make a bowstring from your sinews. You will beg for death, and I will not give it to you. You will pray to your god for mercy, but he will not hear you."

Japheth only spat a gobbet of blood into my father's face in response.

My father placed the point of his spear against Japheth's throat, drawing a pink spot of blood. I saw my father's muscles tense, prepare for the push that would rip open Japheth's neck.

"NO!" I cried out. "Please, Father, no. I'll do anything you ask, just spare him, please."

My father glared at me, put the butt of his spear against the ground, and regarded me, thinking.

"Anything?" He smiled, and it wasn't a pleasant smile.

I knew what he had in mind, and I nearly wept at the thought.

He would marry me to Sin-Iddim, King of Larsa, the most vile man I had ever encountered. Raper of boys and women. Old and saggy of flesh, cunning and vain and cruel . . . and obsessed with me. He had asked my father a dozen times for my hand in marriage, and always I refused. My father had not forced me to marry him up until now, because I was all he has left of my mother, for my brothers all came from different women, and my father loved none of them. He only ever loved my mother—she was most like the human woman Irkalla spoke of, I think, which was why he loved her, why he changed so much after he killed her: it was the only act he had ever regretted.

A marriage between Larsa and Bad-Tibira would bring the two cities a more stable peace, and that was what my father wanted more than anything, as Larsa was the one threat to his reign. The two cities had warred intermittently for centuries, and a peace between them would be a valuable thing, to my father.

Could I marry Sin-Iddim to save Japheth?

Gods save me.

The answer was slow in coming, with my father glaring at me, waiting.

I prayed to The One God in desperation. *Elohim, please. Tell me what to do. If you are the God your followers claim, then you can help me.*

I didn't hear an answer in my mind. There was no voice of prophecy or gods whispering in my ear; I felt only a stillness in my heart, a knowing in my soul—Elohim had other plans for me.

I knew what I would endure for the sake of loving Japheth.

I knew, and I wept.

# CHAPTER 3

## Filled With Violence

"Now the earth was corrupt in God's sight, and
the earth was filled with violence." Genesis
6:11 ESV

Japheth watched as Aresia wept. He didn't
understand completely. All he knew was she was
about to do something to save him, which would
cost her greatly. No one had said what it was, but
King Emmen-Utu and Aresia both seemed to know
without having to put it into words.

"So it is settled," the King said, his voice rumbling like distant thunder.

Aresia didn't speak, only nodded, face buried in
her hands. Japheth forced himself to his feet, desperate to comfort her. She shouldn't save him; he
wasn't worth it.

He stumbled and lurched to her side. "Don't, please." His voice was hoarse and rough. Blood dripped from his face onto the polished floor. "Whatever you're about to do, don't do it. I'll be fine."

She looked down at him through tear-flooded golden eyes, shaking her head. A strand of auburn hair fell loose from the intricate bundle at the nape of her neck, and he reached up to tuck it behind her ear.

"It is done, Japheth, and it cannot be undone." Her gaze left his face, flickered to her father, standing behind Japheth like a mountain of anger and hatred, and then back to him.

She kissed him, a slow, passionate farewell, a kiss deeper and more potent than any they had shared until that moment, a kiss tasting of citrus and garlic, sending a pang of realization through him that drowned out even his pain.

Emmen-Utu grabbed him by the hair and ripped him away. "I'll have his head yet, you stupid girl," he snarled at Aresia. And then he turned to Japheth and kicked him to the floor. "Get you gone, worm, before I change my mind."

Japheth was lifted painfully to his feet by his hair and shoved toward the door. He stumbled and nearly fell, catching himself. At the threshold, he stopped, turned to look at Aresia once more; she had fallen to her knees, face to the floor, shoulders heaving. Japheth wanted to weep at the sight of her torment, and actually took a step back into the throne room, but Emmen-Utu hurled the spear at him, the spearhead burying in the wood door frame beside his face, the shaft shaking and thrumming and wavering side to side.

The day beyond the palace walls was hot and dry, leaching what little strength Japheth had left. The king's guards had given him a severe beating, pummeling him with fists and spear-butts and kicking him with boots; several ribs were cracked, causing sharp lances of pain with every breath and every step. He shuffled slowly away from the palace clutching his side and wanting to do nothing so much as storm back into palace and take Aresia for himself. Sense won out, however—he knew he wouldn't get past the gate alive, and that would do Aresia no good.

He had his small room, let to him by a kindly old man and his wife, candle-makers. He went there, step by dragging step, his thoughts on Aresia and her mysterious sacrifice. What had she done, and why? She was attracted to him, that much was obvious, but mere attraction couldn't explain her actions. She had defied her father for him, had agreed to something she clearly feared more than death itself, all to save him from her father's wrath;

all this, and they barely knew each other.

Japheth had no answers, but the churning in his gut told him he wouldn't like the answers even if he had them. All he could do now was go home and recover.

He was a warrior, and one of some reknown, even among the Nephilim, yet his life had been saved by a woman. A princess, to be sure, but still; her status was little comfort. Especially galling was the fact that he had no idea what she had agreed to in the name of preserving his life. Something horrible, something she feared down to her marrow. He could have done nothing to stop it, but he felt . . . emasculated. Worthless. His pain seemed a fitting price for his guilt.

His room overlooked the main street, giving him a clear view of traffic entering and exiting the city by the main gate. For three days he sat at the window and stared out, lost in thought, despondent and hurting. His landlord's wife had brought him several meals he'd forced himself to eat. The food was tasteless to him, ash in his mouth. The wine had gone down much easier—too well. One wineskin had led to two, and after two his despair had seemed insurmountable, an endless river flowing through his heart, drowning him from within. A third skin had lessened the pang of sorrow, and a fourth left him slumped in a kind of drifting peacefulness, which he knew deep inside was false. He didn't care. The forgetting was his goal, and to that end he continued to drink until he felt nothing at all.

A hand slapped him awake, shook him, jostled him, dragged him from his bed. He cracked an eye and saw a man standing over him, or was it three men? Japheth couldn't tell and didn't care. The spinning ceiling made his stomach lurch, and even with one eye closed he couldn't make out the features of the person above him.

"Get your drunk carcass off the floor, you lazy worm." The gravelly voice, however, was unmistakable: Zidan, mercenary warrior, and Japheth's only friend. "You've been moping about in here for a month, mooning after that Nephilim princess like a lovesick boy. It's time to move on. She was never meant for the likes of you."

Japheth groaned, rubbed his eyes with his palms, struggled to sit up. "Go away, Zidan."

Zidan's fist collided with Japheth's jaw, not a full blow, just enough to hurt. "Be a man, Japheth. You can't keep feeling sorry for yourself. What's done is done, and you can't undo it." He paused for effect. "Aresia is already in Larsa."

That got Japheth's attention. "Larsa? Why is she in Larsa?"

"You don't know?" Zidan sighed. "Well, I guess you may as well hear it from me rather than another—Aresia was married to Sin-Iddim."

Japheth reeled and fell back upon his bed. When he could speak again he said, "Sin-Iddim? Gods damn it all. Him? Of all the kings in Sumer, *him*?"

"Listen," Zidan began, "I know how you feel about him, but—"

"No! You don't know!" Japheth exploded, "You can't know. You weren't there, Zidan, remember? Gods damn it all! It was as if Ereshkigal himself had arisen from the underworld to devour us all. Sin-Iddim had been there in his chariot, commanding the forces from behind the battle lines. Never once did he get within a bow's shot of the action but, by all the gods, his men chewed us up like gristle and spat us out. It wasn't Emmen's fault, I have to give him that, even much as I hate him, especially now. Our forces in the east were overrun, and suddenly, after hours of fighting, we were flanked—it was a slaughter. I remember the moment the Larsan warriors hit us. I heard the crash when the lines hit—you know the sound. Men meeting men, shield against shield, the screams of arms being crushed and legs getting snapped. Larsans, thousands of them, hitting us on the right flank, our weak side. That first clash took out hundreds, easily."

Japheth paused, remembering, and accepted a skin of water from Zidan, swigging, swishing, and spitting to clear his mouth of the taste of dust coating his tongue.

"They didn't kill us outright but captured us instead, at least a thousand of us. They marched us back to Larsa, tied neck to neck. Some they sold as slaves, others they kept and brought to the palace, and I was with the latter group. Sin-Iddim has a taste for torture, even worse than Emmen's. Unlike our fair king, however, Sin-Iddim has the ability to keep them alive. Emmen gets greedy for the kill, so his victims never last long. Sin-Iddim? He's patient and careful. And he likes boys as much as girls. He sodomized some of the male prisoners, right there in the throne room, in front of everyone."

Japheth halted, his throat dry, memories assaulting him. "I vowed to kill myself, or get myself killed before I let that happen to me. He took me from the bunch of prisoners and tortured me for several hours . . . perhaps longer, I don't know. I thought for sure he was going to violate me as he had so many others, and I think he meant to, eventually, but Emmen's messenger arrived before he could get to me. The king had bartered for us: two thousand slaves, a thousand oxen, and some gold for all of the prisoners taken in the battle."

Zidan interrupted, "Why would Emmen barter for a bunch of humans?"

"There weren't many other humans among the prisoners; it was mostly Nephilim. One of Emmen's sons, Dummuzi, was among the prisoners, and he had to get him back without giving away the fact that he was there. No one had noticed, I guess, because it was Dummuzi's first battle, so he hadn't made a name for himself yet, not like Kichu or Algar. Dummuzi was one of the poor bastards Sin-Iddim sodomized, and the boy has never been stable since. It turned him nasty, that experience, and I don't blame him.

"That throne room was awful, Zidan. I thought perhaps I'd been killed after all and had been dragged down to Kur. Emmen keeps a clean court in comparison, I tell you. He kills and tortures, and perhaps tumbles a whore every now and then, but nothing like what went on in the court of Sin-Iddim. That demon sat on his throne the whole while, watching it happen and smiling like he found it delightful. I don't know if Dummuzi ever told his father what happened—I'm not sure even Emmen would marry his daughter to that man if he knew what he was really like."

Zidan looked pale. "I . . . I had no idea, Japheth."

"I know you didn't, Zidan. I don't talk about it much, and now you know why. And you also know why I have to get her back, somehow."

"It's impossible, Japheth. She's a queen now. She's out of your reach, and there's nothing you can do." Zidan hauled Japheth to his feet. "Listen, I've got some work lined up. Come with me, and I'll share the profit with you. It'll be easy—we're escorting a fat old cloth-seller to Ur. We'll break a few heads on the way, find some whores in Ur, and you'll forget all about this fancy Nephilim girl. I promise you."

Japheth just laughed, a joyless bark of sarcasm. "Zidan, I'll never forget her. I can't. I've been trying."

"You've been drinking yourself into a stupor, you idiot. That's not forgetting. The only way to forget a woman is to live on and find another."

"The wisdom of a lecher."

"But I'm never heartsick, am I? Now come on. Urugan is waiting."

Japheth hauled himself to his feet and followed after Zidan, his head throbbing and his heart cracked.

Urugan the cloth-seller was the fattest, shortest man Japheth had ever seen. Barely five feet tall, he was almost completely spherical, tottering about on stubby little legs, waving pudgy arms with busy, gold-ringed fingers. Porcine eyes and fleshy lips gave him the impression of weak-minded stupidity, but Urugan was a wealthy cloth-merchant and anything but stupid. He sat in a little two-wheeled wagon pulled by four large, braying onagers, popping dates in his mouth and shouting for the caravan to move faster—the customers in Ur were waiting. Japheth plodded on foot next to Urugan's wagon, listening to the sweaty little man babble; he kept up a non-stop prattle like a child, commenting on everything he saw, speaking every thought that entered his head, and if Japheth tried to so much as respond, Urugan would throw a date at him.

Zidan had promised this trip would help him forget about Aresia but, so far, all it was doing was depressing him further. Mile after mile on foot, with nothing to do but think about her, remembering their nights together, remembering that last kiss, remembering the way she'd first approached him, swaying her hips, remembering the feel of her arms around him, her golden eyes inches from his as they moved together. Gods, the woman was beautiful . . . too beautiful for an ugly old sodomizing demon like Sin-Iddim. Too beautiful, too good, too kind. Sure she was a little arrogant, but what Nephilim wasn't?

Descended from angels, they claimed to be, and it was possible. Stronger and taller than humans, and longer-lived by far, they were assuredly oth-er-than-human. They ruled the cities, dominated over humans, swaggered like gods and took what they wanted. Unstoppable in battle and brutal in everything they did, the Nephilim indeed seemed like angels made flesh, gods clothed in vileness and evil and selfish conceit. Noah, Japheth's father, claimed that one day Elohim, The One God, would get sick of watching the sins of his once-perfect creation and wipe them all out. Japheth wasn't sure he believed in Elohim any longer, but if He did exist, Japheth earnestly hoped He would wipe out the Nephilim.

Ur was a huge, bustling place with a ziggurat on every corner, dedicated to every god, major and minor, that one could think of. Priests and acolytes shuffled by with their noses in the air, hands clasped importantly behind their backs, expressions of holiness and self-righteousness on their haughty faces. Worshippers ascended long stairways to the temple-tops, offering grain and gold and meat and slaves to the priests in return for blessings of a prosperous season or in propitiation for sins committed, or simply to appease the ever-hungry gods.

Barely-clothed prostitutes swayed up and down the streets, making eyes at any male they saw, offering days and nights of endless pleasure, lifting skirts and pulling aside bodices to display their wares. Guards from the palace patrolled the streets, clashing and scuffling on occasion with temple guards and mercenaries like Zidan and Japheth.

Every street was lined with sellers hawking wares of all kinds, as well as scholars offering to inscribe the customer's name in cuneiform on clay tablets as protection against evil spirits. Japheth had been to other cities around Bad-Tibira, of course, but never as far south as Ur, which was by far the largest city he'd ever seen. It dwarfed Bad-Tibira easily, the walls rising up nearly twice the height and easily twice as thick—making Ur's walls some thirty feet high and ten feet thick—enclosing a population thrice that of his home city.

Japheth was jerked back to reality when Zidan smacked the back of his head, jolting his attention. "Pay attention, farm-boy," he said. "We've got trouble."

Ahead, a troop of temple guards had spread across the road, blocking the way, weapons drawn. Only the royal guards wielded more power and authority than temple guards, who did the bidding of the high priests of the various temples. Temple priests were known in most cities to be brutal and ruthless; most people kept their heads down and prayed hard when temple guards were around, hoping to remain unnoticed.

The lead guard, a massive Nephilim man with a long scar cutting through a thick beard, stepped forward when Urugan and the small band of humans halted.

"Ereshkigal demands a sacrifice," he barked.

His golden glowing eyes scanned the knot of human mercenaries, flicking from one to the other, dismissing each in turn until his gaze settled on Japheth—on his pendant in particular. A cruel smirk twisted his features; he gestured with his spear, pointing at Japheth. "Him."

Before he could even move, the guards rushed Japheth and grabbed his arms, pinioning him between them. Wrestling his spear away, they forced him to his knees. One or two guards Japheth would have fought, but more than a dozen? And more but a shout away?

"But sir, he is not—he is not a slave" Urugan protested, "He is a soldier, one of my loyal guards. Please, give me an hour, and I will personally bring a slave to the temple as sacrifice."

The guard only laughed. "You may bring another, if you wish. Unless you're volunteering to take his place?"

"No—no, sir. Please, take him," Urugan wheedled.

Japheth struggled in vain against the vise-like grip of the guards, and Zidan watched helplessly, not daring to speak up.

His struggles only earned him a brutal blow to the kidney, which rendered Japheth limp and gasping, and from then on he quit struggling, and the guards let Japheth find his feet, guiding him none too gently toward the largest ziggurat in the city. Up a long ramp of stairs they marched him with rough spear-pricks to the back, and with every step the city fell farther away below him, and with it Japheth's hope of getting away from Ur alive.

They brought him into the temple itself, a squat block of stones and sunbaked mud bricks perched at the very top of the ziggurat. Within the ceilings were low and the walls close, the air choking with incense. There were no windows and only the one entrance, which was now a distant rectangle of light.

Priests bustled to and fro within the temple, speaking and praying in low tones, swinging censers and murmuring and chanting; statues of the gods lined the walls, and at the farthest end of the temple stood a likeness of Enlil himself, standing some sixty feet tall and carved to look haughty and stern, one arm outstretched with the palm facing outward and down, as if gesturing for the worshippers to kneel down and pay obeisance. Indeed, when the priest caught Japheth staring, he struck him on the mouth with a fist, his ring ripping open Japheth's lip.

"Avert your eyes from the Lord Enlil!" the priest hissed. "Do not look upon the Lord of Heaven. You are not worthy."

Japheth cast his eyes down, as much to hide his rage as to obey the priest. He was led to a small doorway underneath the statue of Enlil and into a small room, barely more than a cell. There was a chair carved out of the stone of the floor itself. Japheth was thrust roughly into the chair, and chains were manacled to his wrists and appended to the walls so that his arms were stretched out wide, and another set bound his ankles to the legs of the chair.

The guards left and stood outside the doorway to wait. After a few minutes of waiting, a priest entered, an aging man some four cubits tall—short by Nephilim male standards—with the natural brawn of his race but with a wide belly sagging over his belt. He had small, dark eyes glittering with malice, and he wore a sleeveless crimson robe held closed by wide leather belt, upon which was hung a long, curved iron dagger. The priest drew a dagger from his belt and stalked in a circle around Japheth, sharpening the blade on a small whetstone. He halted, leaning close to Japheth, and lifted the pendant off of Japheth's chest with the tip of his knife.

"You wear the name of the false god upon you, little human." The priest spoke in a conversational tone, belying the dangerous zing of steel on stone, the threat of blood to be spilled.

Japheth was beginning to think the pendant his mother had given him was more trouble than it was worth—he'd only insisted upon wearing it out of fondness for his mother, rather than out of any love for Elohim, his father's One God. A few Nephilim gave him trouble about it every now and again, but never anything like this. First Emmen, now this priest . . . all for a god in whom Japheth wasn't even sure he believed in any more. His mother would be hurt deeply if she knew he had taken it off, but it wasn't worth dying over.

"Take it," Japheth said, offering it to him. "Take it, then."

"Ah, so quick to renounce your god, are you? It won't be that easy. No indeed." The priest tossed the pendant aside and then leaned over Japheth. Slowly he dragged the tip of the dagger through the meat of Japheth's chest. Then, casually, he lifted the blade to his lips and licked the blood away with relish. "Where is your One God now? Can your petty *Elohim* save you now, little worm? No indeed." The blade flicked out and the tip of Japheth's ear lobe dropped to the floor. The priest picked it up and ate it, chewing slowly and watching Japheth's reaction all the while.

"What do you want from me?" Japheth stared hard at the priest, refusing to betray pain or disgust.

The priest didn't answer, but instead left the little room and spoke to the Nephilim guards outside. One of them stamped his spear-butt against the floor in a salute and left at a run. Minutes passed slowly, and Japheth felt pain radiating throughout his whole body. He ear throbbed, and he began to feel the strain of being chained as he was, arms stretched so far apart that he had to hold himself up off the chair to ease the pain in his shoulders.

At length, the guard returned, dragging with him a young human girl, a temple prostitute, by the look of her.

She was sobbing and begging, "Please, please— tell me what you want! I'll give it you, I promise. You can have me for free! Please, let me go!"

The guard didn't respond, only laughed cruelly, and thrust the girl into the room with Japheth. The girl shrank into a corner, sobbing hysterically. She obviously knew the priest, and feared him; Japheth was beginning to understand why.

She was young, barely more than a child, clad in only a sheer linen shift, which revealed more than it clothed. Her black hair was intricately braided and her eyes were heavily painted with kohl.

The priest left the room, only to return immediately, a mortar and pestle in his hands. He ground up whatever herbs or seeds the bowl contained, grinding in smooth, practiced movements until he was satisfied with the consistency. He then reached into a pocket in his robe and produced a small clay jar stoppered with a cork. He worked the cork loose and dribbled a small measure of the clear liquid into the bowl, and mixed the contents with the pestle again. Finished, he approached Japheth.

Grasping his jaws in a pincer grip, he forced his mouth open. The old priest's hands were strong enough that Japheth knew if he resisted, the priest would merely break his jaws apart. Giving in with a mental curse, Japheth allowed the priest to place the contents of the bowl upon his tongue. Leaves, mixed with some oil . . . the taste was bitter and potent. He swallowed, feeling no immediate effects.

The priest seemed content to wait in silence, as if he knew exactly what the herbs would do, and how long it would take before the effects could be felt.

And indeed, within a quarter of an hour, by Japheth's mental estimation, he began to feel a stirring between his legs, a rush of blood to his manhood, feeling the organ hardening, a feeling he could not stop, no matter how hard he tried.

The effect of the herbs visibly apparent, the priest nodded, pleased with himself.

He turned to the girl who was huddled in a corner of the room, shivering and shuddering.

"You know who I am, girl?" the priest asked.

"Y-yes, you are Mesh-te, High Priest of Ereshkigal."

"And why are you afraid, girl?"

"They—they say that you . . ." She stopped, afraid to say anything else.

Mesh-te tested the edge of his dagger and gestured for her to continue. "Yes? They say what? You will be punished for disobedience if you do not speak."

The words came out in a rush: "They say you take delight in evil things. They say you watch people lie together and kill them afterward. They say you drink human blood and eat human flesh. Oh, Inanna, save me! They say such awful things, your grace. But I do not believe them! A priest would not be so evil, surely."

"Oh girl, if only you knew." Mesh-te laughed, knelt down beside her, dagger at her chin. "Yes, girl, much of what the rabble says about me is true, and more besides. So . . . you will do as I tell you, won't you?"

"Oh, yes, your grace! Please, tell me what you wish me to do!" She was shaking, poor thing. Blood was trickling down her throat from where the knife-tip pressed against her flesh.

Mesh-te gestured at Japheth. "He is a worshipper of The One God. He needs to be shown how to worship our gods, the *real* gods. You understand? I wish you to perform your duties as an acolyte of Inanna."

The girl paled, whimpered. "But, your grace, I am not an acolyte, only a humble temple prostitute."

"All the better! He wishes to worship Inanna,

and you, whore, will help him." The girl didn't move, and Mesh-te leaned in close, hissing in his serpent's rasp. "The longer you wait, the more harshly I will treat you."

Japheth understood what Mesh-te was demanding, and it sickened him. "There's no need for this," he said. "Let the girl go. Torture me if you wish."

"I told you it wouldn't be that easy. If you cause trouble, I will punish the girl." He stood up, lashed out with a fist and struck the girl on the face, knocking her to the ground, glancing at Japheth as the girl dabbed at the blood trickling from her nose. "That was for questioning me. Do you have any more to say?"

Japheth shook his head, and the girl stifled a sob as the priest hauled her to her feet and shoved her toward Japheth. With a swift slice of his dagger, the priest cut open Japheth's tunic from neck to hem, the razor sharp edge parting the thick leather of his belt easily. The garment fell open, revealing Japheth's arousal, which he was still fighting against, futilely.

The prostitute glanced at the priest, who merely grinned, and then she looked back at Japheth.

"I'm sorry," she whispered.

"It's because of me that you're here, girl," Japheth murmured. "Do what you must."

She climbed astride him, seating him inside her, and began moving her hips, grinding against him, but Japheth felt no desire for a mere slip of a girl as this—even under normal circumstances he wouldn't have desired her. His desires were irrelevant however; the herbs the priest had forced him to swallow had seen to that.

The girl moved on him, and Japheth fought against the physical response of his body to her touch. But then . . . if she couldn't do as the priest wished, Mesh-te might hurt her further, and it would Japheth's fault. The priest, watching, was licking his lips and fondling himself, as if watching gave him as much pleasure as performing the act himself.

Japheth closed his eyes and stopped fighting his physical response to her touch, wanting to pray for forgiveness, but unwilling to believe in any god who could allow such evil in the world. She knew her trade all too well, this girl, and Japheth struggled against the riot of mixed emotions, pleasure and pain, hatred and disgust. He opened his eyes and met her gaze and saw the apology there. He needed to feel something besides her movement upon him, so he pulled against the chains with all his strength, straining until the manacles cut into the flesh of his wrist, providing a stinging counterpoint of pain to balance against what the girl was doing—

Suddenly a hot wet rush burst over Japheth's face and chest, filling his mouth with an sickly-sweet tang, a sharp taste he knew all too well, and the girl whose name he never knew gasped in surprise and gurgled and thrashed above him. Japheth opened his eyes and saw the prostitute on top of him, her robes fallen open, head tipped back, dark hair cascading around pale shoulders . . . a scarlet gash across her throat. Blood ran down her flesh, coating her breasts crimson. He reached for her, wanting to ease her passage somehow, but the chains prevented him and he could only cry out in rage, spitting out her blood.

Mesh-te the demon-priest was licking the blood from the blade of his dagger, grinning, pleased, aroused.

Japheth, turned his head away, closed his eyes, horror searing through him.

*Elohim, why do you allow this?* Japheth found himself praying to his father's god for the first time in so long, turning to The One God for some kind of comfort in his agony. *Elohim, if you are real, if you are The One God—*

Japheth was going to ask Elohim to end his suffering, but he found himself thinking of Aresia instead, and changed his prayer: *Elohim, spare her. Spare Aresia. Protect her, if you are The One True God. Let me suffer instead of her.*

Eventually the priest staggered from the room, the girl's body now empty of blood.

The next hours blended together until Japheth

couldn't have said if he'd been chained to the chair for hours or days, or if he had ever been free, if he had ever seen the sunlight, or tasted wine upon his lips, or felt the wind on his face.

# CHAPTER 4

## Bone of My Bones

"Then the man said, 'This at last is bone of my
bones and flesh of my flesh; she shall be called
Woman, because she was taken out of man.'"
Genesis 2:23 ESV

ONCE AGAIN MY DAYS AND NIGHTS WERE FILLED
with the sound of screams. The court of King
Sin-Iddim was worse than Father's, by far. Some
of the screams were howls of agony drawn from
tortured captives, others were moans of pleasure
from the pairs or groups of people mating on the
floors and couches scattered throughout the throne
room.

I sat on my throne next to my new husband and
stared at the sliver of blue sky visible through the
far doorway. A slave cowered at my feet, a human

boy not yet old enough to grow a beard, naked, crusted with dirt and scabs and dried blood, hair matted and tangled, chains on his feet and hands. He knelt on all fours, face pressed against the floor, waiting. I had learned he would not rise from that position unless commanded by the King. Even if struck or kicked by a guard or priest or courtier, the boy would remain motionless and silent. I wished I could kneel beside him, scrub away the dirt and blood, send him to play in the streets with the other boys his age. I knew, however, even if I did, he would have no concept of play, no notion of fun. The one time his eyes met mine I had seen no life there, no identity in his gaze, and only a lifeless apprehension of pain.

The only kindness I could perform for him would be to plunge a dagger into his heart—he would welcome that. Oh, Inanna, what was the world coming to, that an innocent boy's life should be so awful? The boy served only one function . . . he was not a cupbearer, not a spear-bearer, not a servant of any kind—his only role in life was to be sodomized by the king.

There was no concept of privacy in the court of Sin-Iddim. Whenever the mood took him, the king would rise from his throne, grab the boy by the hair, bend him over and violate him, right on the throne, in front of anyone who happened to be watching.

He hadn't done that particular evil to me yet, thank the gods, but it was coming, and soon. I had expected Sin-Iddim to take me to his bedchamber the moment we arrived at the palace, but he hadn't. His first act was to rape the boy, watching me as he did so with a vile glint in his eyes. He was playing with me, I knew. He wanted me to wait, wanted me to dread what was coming.

And I did—I dreaded it with all of my soul.

Sin-Iddim was an old man, nearly twice my father's age. His black hair and beard were shot with silver, his skin tanned nearly black, wrinkled and weathered and taut against his bones like stretched leather. He would have been a powerful and attractive man in his youth, for even in his old age he was strong and energetic and restless. His eyes were the color of burnished copper lit by the sun, always in motion, roving, roving, and penetrating in their intensity, hungry for gore and violence and rapine.

He had arrived within a week of my father's messenger, striding into the palace as if he owned it. He'd dropped a sack of gold and jewels at my father's feet, grabbed me by the arm, his eyes glinting with eagerness and malice, silently promising me nights of endless hell. My father had called for a scribe to carve the terms of the treaty into a tablet, and they both had signed it with their name-rune. Then my father watched me leave with an impassive expression on his face.

Yet . . . was that a glint of regret I saw in his eyes as I left his palace? It didn't seem possible, and I doubted I had seen it.

The trip had been long and dusty, and Sin-Iddim's hands had groped me for much of it, which I endured in silence. He hadn't spoken a word. I was thankful for Irkalla's presence beside me, the one comfort from home I had been allowed to bring with me. She held my hand, squeezing it at times to express her sympathy.

I tried not to think of Japheth. Tried not to wonder where he was, or if he thought of me.

As it did every night, dusk fell upon the court of the King of Larsa. I loathed the coming of night. On the nineteenth day of my marriage to Sin-Iddim, after the last of the courtiers had gone and the slaves were chained to the pillars and the warriors returned to barracks, my husband the King demanded my presence. There was no preamble, no pretense of affection or even kindness. He merely pushed me into his bedchamber, threw me against the tall, hand-carved bed-frame and told me to strip.

*Inanna, help me.* My hands trembled, and my legs shook; I hesitantly began tugging at the ties of my gown. Not quickly enough, it seemed, for Sin-Iddim cursed, drew his knife, and cut away the straps, gouging my shoulder in the process. The dress fell to the floor, and I was left standing naked before him. I tried to cover myself with my hands, but he knocked my hands away.

"No need for modesty, girl," he grunted. "You belong to me now."

Against my will, tears welled in my eyes.

I was helpless against him. He shoved me to the bed, hands squeezing my breasts with bruising fingers, forcing apart my knees . . .

I bled, and whimpered—and received a vicious blow to the mouth to silence me. Irkalla wept in the corner, her face turned away, shoulders shaking.

Thus began my marriage to Sin-Iddim, King of Larsa, and so it continued, every night in the weeks that followed.

One afternoon a messenger, a curly-haired Nephilim boy breathless from running, arrived from my father. "My lord King . . . news from Ur."

"What is it, boy? Spit it out."

The messenger quaffed from a skin of water brought by a servant, and then continued between gasps. "Uruk has attacked Ur, my lord . . .

they arrived at dawn yesterday with twenty thousand foot soldiers and . . . and ten thousand chariots. King Emmen-Utu requests that you bring your forces and meet him at the walls of Uruk. He—he says that together you can take the city while the army is gone."

The king's eyes lit up with greed: Uruk was the second largest city after Ur, and filled with wealth. "If Uruk falls to us," Sin-Iddim said, "and if Ur falls to Argandea of Uruk, then we will be unstoppable. Argandea will be weak from battle, and we will have both cities."

"Yes, my lord." the messenger said. "That is his plan."

"Shut up, boy. I wasn't talking to you." The king turned to a middle-aged warrior standing next to him, a general by the looks of him. "Lugash—call up the troops. Prepare for war." The general nodded and left the chamber.

The king ran his fingers through his beard, lost in thought, and I prayed to Inanna to keep my husband gone for many months, and I begged Ninurta to strike down my husband, that I might be a widow. By dusk the next day the army was tromping out of the city, the king at their head. I was so glad to see him go that I offered a sacrifice to Inanna; I made a bargain with her as smoke from the burnt offering coiled up to heaven: if she took my husband, I would bring a burnt offering to her temple every week for a month.

Irkalla stood with me on the roof of the palace, watching the stream of soldiers depart, spears glinting in the sun, dust from the road rising like a cloud. "Are you well, mistress?" Her voice was heavy with worry.

"Well enough, I suppose. Better now that he's gone."

"I hope he dies in battle," Irkalla said. "I hope he takes a spear to the gut and dies slowly and in pain."

"Hush, Irkalla! His servants are everywhere. If they report your words to him, even I can't save you."

"I would rather die than remain here in his service another moment." She leaned in close and lowered her voice to a fierce whisper. "Let us leave, my lady. Let us flee! With all the chaos around us, now is the time. If we leave in the night, we can be far away before anyone notices we are gone. I have a brother in Eridu, he will take us in."

I shook my head. "No, Irkalla. The king would find us, and then he would raze Eridu to the ground. He would torture your brother to death, and rape his corpse. No. You go, but I cannot. I cannot be the cause of anyone else's pain."

"Blood of the gods," Irkalla cursed, "you are so stubborn. You saved that human, Japheth, by marrying this demon. Now, save yourself. You can pretend to be a servant. Cut off your hair. Rub dirt on your face. Roll in manure and bathe in mud—no one would know you as a queen or princess, then. I can disguise you, I can hide you, teach you to act like a common girl, like a slave. Please, Aresia! Run away now, while he is gone. You won't get another chance."

"No, Irkalla. I will not. I would flee to the underworld itself, if it meant escaping that vile creature, but he would find us anywhere we went—I *know* it. He would kill anyone who helped us, and he would kill you and your family, your mother and father and your sisters and their husbands and their children. He is a monster, and he would stop at nothing."

She fell silent then, knowing I would not be moved. I wanted desperately to flee, as she suggested, but I could not stomach the thought of anyone dying for me; I would stay in Larsa and accept my fate. Perhaps I could make him kill me one day and end my suffering that way.

A month after my husband left, I began to feel sick in the mornings and my courses stopped; for all his age, the king was still virile. Irkalla noticed as well, and called a healer, an ancient Nephilim woman, stooped and gray and wrinkled, one eye blind, teeth rotted, fingernails long and curling over, her body sagging. She shuffled into my chamber, leaning on a short staff, a bag of herbs in one hand.

"With child, you are." She hadn't even examined me before making the pronouncement. "King's child. Come, girl, let me look at you." She poked and prodded, hemmed and nodded and muttered to herself.

"I know I am pregnant, old woman."

"Then what do you want with old Mirra? Hmmm? If you don't summon me to tell you this, you want something else." Her one rheumy brown eye fixed on me, and the healer shuffled close enough that I could smell the garlic and onions on her breath. "Perhaps you want some different herbs, eh? Not so grateful for this gift of the king, perhaps? Ah, girl, I've heard the stories. I know the ways of the king. I've been summoned to heal the boys he's used, and the slave girls as well. More than one bastard child runs the streets of Larsa, unwanted. Yes, girl, I know why you called me."

"Then give me the herbs that will take the child back to the gods."

"Forgive me, mistress, but I cannot. The king would know I've been to you, and he knows the herbs I'd use. He's a cunning king, that man. If I do what you ask, it would be my head. Old I may be, but I am not ready to meet Ereshkigal, not yet."

I wept, then. "Please—please. I will have you

taken to my father's city. I can have you protected, there."

Mirra shook her head. "No, girl. If the gods will it, the child will live, and the child will die by their will."

I clutched her hand, falling to my knees before her. "I cannot have that monster's child! I cannot. I would rather die. Give me poison then."

Mirra pulled me up. "Just because the father is a demon, does not mean the child will be. I cannot give poison to the queen. You know that. The guards watch, and they report."

I shoved Mirra away, roughly, and she stumbled back against the wall. "Fine then," I hissed. "Leave me to my fate."

"I'm sorry, child . . . I wish I could give you what you want. I was married to a man I didn't love, once. I know your pain."

"You don't know my pain," I snapped. "Maybe you were married to a man you didn't love, but did he do what Sin-Iddim does? Did your husband rape you every night? Did he rape you so hard you bled, even though it's not your moon-cycle? Did he sodomize little boys in front of you?"

Mirra glared at me, her eyes hard and ancient and unforgiving. She was not intimidated by me, not at all. Her eyes pierced me, sifted through my soul.

"Bah! What do you know of pain, girl?" Mirra's voice crackled, as hard as her eyes. She'd seen a hundred lifetimes, her eyes said to me; she'd seen things I could never imagine. "You know *nothing*. I was not always a stooped and haggard old crone, you know. Once, my back was straight, my hair was dark and thick like yours, and my hips were round like yours and my breasts high like yours. Once, I was beautiful, like you. Once, I was proud, like you and thought I knew everything, like you. Once, I loved a man, like you do."

A twisted grin curled the wrinkled corners of her mouth.

"Yes, girl, I know your secret," she cackled. "I see what you hide from the king. I see what you hide even from yourself . . . yes, girl, I see it. You cannot hold secrets from old Mirra. Come, sit. Yes, sit here, next to me, and listen. Hear the wisdom of an old hag who has seen a dozen lifetimes."

I had little better to do but wait, so I sat beside Mirra and listened to her story.

"When I was young and nubile and beautiful," Mirra began, "I loved a man. He was tall, and strong. He was handsome and virile. He kissed me, and the world stopped. He held me, and the stars sang for our love. But the gods—and my father— had other plans for me. You see, my father was a wealthy man, a merchant. There was another man, another merchant just as wealthy as my father who dealt in the same goods, cloth and spices and slaves, and he ran his goods along the same trade routes as my father. You are a smart girl, I'm sure you can see where this led. Two proud, wealthy men plying the same goods along the same route . . . they came to blows more than once.

"Then, one day, the other merchant happened to see me. I was walking with my servants, coming home from the market. I remember what I wore that day—two hundred years ago or more it was, but I remember the deep indigo of the dress, the richness of the fabric as it lay against my skin, the kohl thick on my eyes, gold on my wrists and opals on my neck. My hips swayed like rushes in the wind, and my hair was piled atop my head in intricate braids. Every man in the market saw me, and every man desired me. Sannin was no different, although he was old, older than my father by a dozen years at least. I had no eyes for him—he might as well have been a wall or an urn for all that I noticed him. I only had eyes for my lover.

"He was a no one, my Jorin. His father was a poor carpenter, and Jorin had only a spear and a shield to his name, but he was a strong and fierce warrior . . . he was a god, in my eyes, for all that he was poorer than the very dirt underfoot.

"But you know what happens, yes? My father

102

had a brilliant plan. He enticed Sannin to a tavern, plied him with wine, spoke to him of the merits of joining forces, doing business together. My father had a way with words, and he sold Sannin on the idea. But Sannin had one condition. He would only do business with my father if he could have me as his wife. My father never even batted an eyelash. He agreed right there, without so much as speaking to my mother, much less to me.

"He wouldn't hear a word from me about what I wanted or didn't want. I didn't matter. I was given to Sannin like a bolt of linen, and for less than that in bride-price. Less than a month passed between the meeting and the wedding. I wept all that day. Sannin, old as he was, still had plenty of sap left in his tree, let me tell you. He plowed my field with all the vigor of a man a hundred years younger, and with all the gentility of an aurochs in full charge. So yes, girl, I know what it's like to bleed after a man's been between my thighs."

Mirra paused, staring into the past, seeing ghosts.

"Sannin had a temper on him," she resumed. "He had quick fists, and he didn't care a whit if I was in his wife, or a servant. My eye was black and blue more often than not. When I was married to Sannin, Jorin, my lover, was furious. He'd been saving his earnings to pay the price for my hand. He'd saved every single coin he'd earned, my sweet Jorin. He starved himself to marry me. Then, just as he was about to ask for my hand, Father married me off to Sannin.

"Jorin didn't take that sitting down, I'll tell you. Sannin went on frequent journeys to other cities, selling his goods, and Jorin, crafty, stupid Jorin, he cornered me in the marketplace. I tried to avoid him, tried to be a dutiful wife. But I couldn't help it. Jorin, he was . . . oh, he smelled of sweat and dust and all things male as his arms crushed me against him. I couldn't help myself. I met him in the market as often as I could, at first merely talking, kissing behind the rug-seller's wares, snatching a moment or two.

"Then, one day Jorin laid me down on a blanket on the floor of a dirty little room and he loved me there, hard and fierce and desperate. He loved me as I've never been loved before or since. I got with child from that, and my husband found out. He was not a stupid man, my husband. He never confronted me about it. He waited, and he watched. He saw me with Jorin, and then he hired a dozen men." Another rife pause. "Jorin died a horrible death. He bled out in the dust outside our home, and I couldn't go to him. Sannin tied me to a chair and sat me facing the window, forced me to watch as my lover and the father of my baby was beaten to death by a dozen men with clubs. Then Sannin turned to me and beat me until I miscarried the baby. When I'd bled the child out, Sannin dragged me through the streets of the city by my hair and tossed me at my father's doorstep and left me there.

"My father wouldn't take me in—he closed the door in my face. My mother snuck out and helped me to a healer, an old woman much as I am now. That old woman saved my life and let me live with her, taught me all she knew, and I became a healer. I've not tasted the sweat on a man's body since Jorin died, and I don't miss it. Jorin was my one love, and he is gone."

She fixed her one rheumy eye on me and pierced me with her sharp, knowing gaze. "So yes, child, I do know exactly what your pain feels like, and more yet that I hope you'll never know." She nodded firmly. "This I know, child: you *will* survive this."

Mirra fell silent, but she didn't take her eyes from me. She took my hand in hers, and her skin felt like dried papyrus that had set out in the sun too long; she smelled of a hundred kinds of herb, and she had a whisker on her chin, dangling from a mole.

"How will I survive?" I whispered. "*How?* He is a monster . . . and this child will be a monster. I can feel it growing, I can feel in my bones that if I bear this child, it will be more evil than the father. He will be like my father and my husband combined . . . I—I cannot. I *cannot*."

Mirra didn't answer. She shook her head, muttered to herself, too low for me to hear. She patted my hand, heaved herself to her feet, leaning on her staff. She took up her bag of herbs and stood over the cup of wine that sat near my elbow. With one long, sad glance at me, Mirra dipped her fingers into the bag and withdrew a pinch of herbs and crushed them into the wine with strong, trembling fingers. She handed the goblet to me and watched me drink it, then placed the bag in Irkalla's hands.

"You know what to do, child," Mirra said to Irkalla. "You have seen this done before, so you know. Be careful to not give her too much, or she could die." A long, long pause, and then Mirra turned her gaze to me. "The gods have granted me a vision of you, girl," she said. "You have a purpose yet, and so you cannot die. You will know the love of your man, but not until you have suffered much."

Her last words chilled the blood in my veins: "Before this demon is loosed from your womb, you will wish for death."

I drank the wine. It was bitter and tasted of oils and herbs and death. My stomach cramped and clenched and my bowels turned to water. Irkalla mixed the wine again the next day and the day after that. Every day the pain worsened, until I could not move from my bed; I screamed until my voice was raw and ragged, and then I screamed silently.

Still the child remained in my womb.

Irkalla mixed the wine again and again. I prayed to every god I knew—save one—for the child to die. It *was* a child—I made no equivocation about that. What I did was as much murder as if I had stabbed it with a knife, but what I had told Mirra was true: this child was a demon, a monster. I could not, would not, bear the child of that evil king.

After a week of unbearable agony, my loins burst open and clots of blood and tissue flooded the bed beneath me in crimson, stinking waves. If I could have screamed aloud, the sound of my voice would have carried to my father's ears, hundreds of miles away. As it was, all that emerged from my throat was dry, rasping gasps; all the agony that had gone before was as the trickle of a stream before a flash flood. The pain that I had endured in the preceding seven days was nothing, nothing at all compared to what I experienced at that moment.

I wept hot silent tears and begged Ereshkigal to take me.

I begged Enki and Enlil to take me.

Finally, when I had pleaded with and cried out

to all the gods of my people, I begged Elohim to forgive me.

All I received from all the gods and from The One God was silence.

The child had no name, no grave. Irkalla burned the effluvia in an urn beneath a window, sprinkling sage on the crackling, foul-smelling flames to dull the scent of burning blood.

The following week, Mirra's head was brought to me in a wicker basket by a grim-faced guard.

# CHAPTER 5

## Wipe Them Out

> "So God said to Noah, 'I have decided to
> destroy all living creatures . . . yes, I will wipe
> them all out along with the earth!'" Genesis
> 6:13 (NLT)

HANDS FUMBLED AT THE MANACLES BINDING
Japheth to the wall.

Japheth ignored them, thinking them hallucina-
tions or dreams. Exhaustion, hunger, and thirst had
sapped his strength, but not nearly so much as the
disgust and horror of the temple prostitute's death.
Japheth had thought himself fairly desensitized
to gore and death from a lifetime of making war,
but the girl . . . he could still taste her blood in his
mouth, could still see her eyes fly wide with shock
and pain as her life fountained out of the gash in her

throat to bathe him crimson. Those weren't what caused the nightmares though. What Japheth saw every time his eyes closed was the face of the priest and the black flood of possession spreading through his eyes, occluding the whites and pupils and irises, until there was naught but black shadow in his gaze.

The hands pulled at Japheth, and a voice buzzed in his ear, but the words were dull and distant and unintelligible. Pain cracked through Japheth's face as a fist connected with his cheek and sent him spinning to slump against the wall.

"Get up, you fool!" Japheth heard Zidan's voice whispering furiously in his ear. "They'll find us in a moment, so if you want to be free of this house of hell, you'd best get moving."

The throbbing in his cheek cleared the haze from Japheth's mind. He blinked his eyes and staggered to his feet; the body of the temple prostitute was still lying on the floor, her eyes wide and glassy, the blood dried in a sticky pool around her body. Japheth knelt and tried to shut her eyes, but she'd been dead too long. Instead, he tore a strip of cloth from the hem of her dress and laid it across her face.

*Take her soul unto yourself, Elohim,* Japheth prayed. *She did not deserve this death.*

"Leave the whore," Zidan growled, "We have to go, now."

Japheth span and thrust his face into Zidan's,

eyes blazing. "She died so that demon-priest could send me a message. Show some respect."

Zidan was unfazed by Japheth's fury. "You'll join her in the afterlife, if we don't leave. I could only buy so much time, and it's nearly gone."

Zidan tossed a guardsman's dirty tunic at him, and then thrust the hilt of an iron short sword into Japheth's left hand and a small buckler into his right. Not waiting for an answer, the mercenary crept out of the antechamber and through the darkened temple. A lone torch flickered on a far wall, and the air was blessedly clear of incense.

Japheth got dressed and grabbed his weapons. Just as he was about the follow Zidan out the door, a glint of something on the floor caught his eye: his pendant. He caught it up and, in doing so, felt an energy course through his body. Maybe Elohim was watching him after all.

The temple wasn't deserted; Japheth could see priests and temple guards roaming along the walls. From behind a thick pillar came a low, feminine moaning and a porcine grunting, and as they passed the pillar Japheth saw pale buttocks flashing with desperate thrusts in the gloom. The pig-snorts of pleasure escalated to a final, feral growl, and the priest dismounted the prostitute, who snatched a handful of coins and scurried out of the temple.

The priest lowered his robe and cast a furtive

glance around the temple, allowing Japheth a brief look at his face in the midnight darkness: Mesh-te.

Japheth's blood boiled, and rage tightened his grip on the short sword. Before Zidan could stop him, Japheth was skulking behind the evil priest. The priest was oblivious to Japheth's presence behind him until it was too late. Japheth lunged like a pouncing lion, one hand clamping around the priest's mouth, the short sword lifting to press against his jowled throat.

"Where are your false gods now, priest?" Japheth rasped. The priest grunted and thrashed, but Japheth was far more powerful than the spent old Nephilim. Japheth dragged sharpened iron across papery flesh, holding Mesh-te still until his flailing stopped. Japheth dropped the corpse to the floor and rejoined Zidan in the main hallway, the entire process having taken less than a minute.

"Feel better?" Zidan asked.

Japheth watched blood drip from the tip of his sword. "No, but it's a start."

Zidan only snorted in reply.

Outside the temple, the city was sleeping, dark and quiet and moonlit. Japheth noticed for the first time Zidan's temple-guard uniform, which explained how they'd managed to walk out without trouble. Zidan was hurrying Japheth down the ziggurat steps and onto the main thoroughfare, getting them as far away from the temple as possible. Mesh-te's body would be discovered soon, and the farther away Zidan and Japheth were, the better. They rounded a corner and Zidan paused to discard the temple-guard uniform, keeping the spear, a rectangular shield, and a breastplate, which he gave to Japheth.

"Now what?" Japheth asked.

"Now we rejoin the fat little merchant and go back to Bad-Tibira with the sunrise."

Japheth finished buckling the breastplate and leaned back against the wall, suddenly tired as the adrenaline left him. "For you, maybe."

Zidan shook his head, yanked Japheth back into a fast walk. "Boy, you are a bigger fool than I thought. You cannot honestly think you can rescue your Nephilim princess, do you? She's a queen, now! And not just any queen, but Sin-Iddim's queen. You fought against the old demon—you know the kind of forces he's got. What do you think you could do alone against an army?"

Zidan shoved Japheth against the wall and held him there by the throat, fury in his eyes.

"I did *not* save you from that gods-damned priest to have you throw your life away for a Nephilim, whether she's a princess, a queen, or a commoner," Zidan said. "She's gone, Japheth! There's nothing you can do."

Japheth slapped Zidan's hand away, then slammed the butt of the spear into the dust, cursing. "Don't you think I know that? You think I meant to fall in love with a Nephilim girl? Gods . . . I thought I'd tumble her a time or two, and she'd be gone. I killed for her, and I would again. If I have to, I will wade through a river of corpses to get to her."

Zidan was silent for once, seeing the dangerous light in Japheth's eyes. Knowing he had no other choice, he stepped aside and let Japheth go and meet his fate.

Larsa seemed small and shabby compared to the mammoth grandeur of Ur. Zidan had given him some coin, and Japheth had spent a few nights in an inn regaining his strength and then had joined a caravan heading to Larsa. He had no real plan, only an unformed notion of trying to get close enough to Sin-Iddim to try and kill him. It was a suicide mission, but it was all he could think of. He'd heard rumors of war in the inn's common room and the other guards in the caravan confirmed that Ur had indeed sent an army against Uruk. That didn't necessarily mean Larsa would get involved, but even being in the same city meant he might be able to formulate some sort of plan. And, if nothing else, joining the Larsan army meant work, which meant a distraction.

So, as the caravan approached the walls of Larsa, Japheth took his leave of the caravan and found the gate captain.

Japheth rattled the hilt of the second-hand short sword in its scabbard at his right hip, wishing for the thousandth time he had his sappara back, but wishes were futile, so he had to content himself with promises to buy one as soon as he could. Short swords and spears were fine, but they didn't suit him, not like the sappara.

A brawny Nephilim gate-captain stopped Japheth with a lowered spear. "What's your business?"

"I'm here to join the King's army," Japheth replied.

"Have you fought before, little man?" The gate-captain was easily three feet taller than Japheth, with arms thicker than Japheth's waist.

"I've fought for Bad-Tibira, Uruk, and Kutallu," Japheth answered, truthfully.

"A mercenary," the Nephilim spat the word like a curse. "Well, I know His Majesty always needs bodies to fill the front ranks, and I suppose you'll do. Ask for Ulun at the barracks, down that way." The guard jerked a thumb to show the direction meant.

Japheth nodded and set off.

Aresia was lost to him and, as Zidan had told him countless times, there was no way to get her back. He hadn't been home in more than seven years, and he doubted his family even thought of him anymore. He could admit to himself that there had been a few times when he'd considered returning home, especially when work was scarce and his belly empty. But even the desire to see his beloved mother, Zara, was not enough for him to stomach the idea of groveling before Noah the righteous, Noah the unbendable.

Japheth did miss his mother though. She'd always been the one to soften Noah's harsh and unforgiving ways, and although she never subverted her husband, she always managed to find ways around his dictatorial edicts and immovable morals; Zara was kind and sweet, and still beautiful despite her age.

Japheth found the barracks quickly, dismissing thoughts of home and his parents, standing rigid and silent as he waited for the mercenary troop captain to make his decision. A few questions about battles and fighting styles had Ulun convinced that Japheth wasn't a novice. He was assigned to a phalanx of other mercenary humans, all destined to be front-rank battle fodder whenever the time came.

As he set about getting a bunk and securing the proper equipment, he heard the other men discussing the coming orders. Japheth had noticed a sense of urgency in the barracks—men were sharpening blades, polishing mail, repairing footwear and rolling cloaks, packing pouches with extra rations of food; they were preparing for war.

"What's happening?" Japheth asked the man nearest him.

"New, eh?" The man was short and barrel-chested, with a hard, round gut and two fingers missing from his left hand. "Uruk attacked Ur yesterday, so our glorious king—forever may he reign—has joined forces with Emmen-Utu of Bad-Tibira. We're going to take Uruk while it's empty of its best soldiers. Seems a cowardly tactic, but I don't make the decisions."

Japheth was stunned. He'd just left that city a week ago, and he wondered if Zidan and the merchant had left before the attack; behind the walls of a besieged city was not a good place to be.

He cursed under his breath—he'd inadvertently joined a war. His chances of getting to Sin-Iddim were now less than nil. He'd joined the Larsan army, and he couldn't very well renege now. Like all the other soldiers, he began to gear up.

Perhaps in the heat of battle he'd be able to forget Aresia.

As it turned out, Uruk hadn't sent their entire army to Ur.

The Larsan army had spent two days gearing up, gathering supplies, readying the supply trains, and organizing for the march, and then had spent another week marching to Uruk.

A day's march from Uruk, scouts had returned claiming that forces were waiting for them outside Uruk, but their total numbers were unknown. What was supposed to be an easy raid on an empty city had suddenly turned into something much, much worse. Japheth was in the very first line of human warriors as the Larsan army approached Uruk.

Dust kicked up under his feet, and his fist ached from clenching his shield strap so tightly. Heat blasted from the sun, bright overhead, sending sweat trickling down his temple and making the haft of his spear slippery in his grip.

About a league from the city walls of Uruk, a massive line of Nephilim warriors waited for them, spears bristling between man-high rectangular shields. Sunlight glistened off burnished helmets and polished mail. Except for the tramp of sandaled feet, silence reigned.

Sin-Iddim hadn't accompanied the foray all the way to the battlefield outside Uruk's walls, instead setting up a royal tent a few leagues away, sending his most senior general, a massive, dour Nephilim named Dagan. The Larsan general did not slow his army when he sighted the line waiting for them. He merely assessed the situation, ordered the siege equipment to stay back, and called the charge.

Fear clamped down on his bowels as he jogged beside his line-mates. The man to his left smelled of piss, and the man on the other side looked ready to break formation any moment. Japheth roared a wordless battle-cry and began running slowly, knowing the rest would follow. On the field of battle, men needed only an example to find their own courage. The entire line sped forward to keep up with him, the line ragged and uneven, wide gaps between shields, and that was when he realized the entire front line was made of green recruits.

This would be a slaughter.

Japheth found himself calling on Elohim for protection, even though he had been trying to convince himself he didn't believe in his father's One God. *Protect me, Elohim, if you are listening.*

That was all the prayer he had time for before the two front lines met with a thunderous clash of metal and flesh and bone and screams. Both of the men beside him died in the first clash.

Immediately prior to the moment of impact, Japheth thrust his huge rectangular shield in front of him and couched his spear in his armpit, leaning forward into his shield and keeping his head behind it, his center of balance low. His whole body juddered as he collided with the opposite line; his spear shook and jumped in his grip, and he heard a wet squish and a grunt of expelled breath. Japheth bashed forward with his shield and yanked his spear backward, hearing a dull wet sucking sound as the blade was released by flesh.

Sweat stung his eyes, and Japheth wiped it away with a forearm, glancing around him to assess the battle. Sin-Iddim had mustered five thousand warriors, which only represented a quarter of his total army's strength; he hadn't seen the necessity of sending every available man, since Uruk was supposed to be mostly empty of soldiers. The king of Uruk, however, had foreseen a potential ambush and had left behind what seemed to Japheth's practiced eye to be nearly three thousand warriors. Uruk was outnumbered, but those few warriors left behind were the cream of Uruk's crop, the doughtiest, hardiest, most seasoned soldiers, and they were acquitting themselves with a vengeance. Withing minutes, it was obvious that even though Larsa had the advantage of numbers, those bodies were mostly green and unseasoned by battle, and were quickly and easily hewn down by their more experienced opponent. Emmen-Utu's army had joined the fray, turning the tide against Uruk; the battle was far from over, however.

Four Nephilim warriors charged at him across the killing field, one of them a full head taller than the rest, making him truly giant even by Nephilim standards. Japheth's heart stopped and his blood ran cold—one he could manage, maybe even two, but not four. He felt a presence beside him and turned to see Kichu standing next to him.

Kichu grinned, a lopsided, feral snarl. "Let's send them to Erishkigal, shall we?"

Japheth felt a rush of relief at Kichu's presence; he had no love for any Nephilim, but Kichu was as close to a friend among them as he had. He'd fought against Larsa next to Kichu, and they had saved each other's lives several times. Japheth nodded at Kichu, swung his sappara in a circle, and tightened his grip on his shield.

Kichu and Japheth stood side by side, a few meters between them. Kichu held an axe in each hand, swinging both at the same time in a scissor cut, one high, the other low, striking so fast Kichu's opponent couldn't track both strikes and took an axeblade to thigh. A single backward step accompanied a third swing, and the Uruk warrior was beheaded. Kichu swiveled sideways to dodge a spear thrust, hacked an axe down at the shaft, splintering it, and swung his other axe in a backhand blow.

Japheth's attention was torn away from Kichu's deadly dance as he warded off blows from two opponents. He dodged and blocked with shield and sword, waiting for an opening and trying to split the pair of warriors. These two were seasoned warriors, however, and refused to be parted. Blow after blow rained down on Japheth's shield, and his left arm was beginning to ache; he had to go on the offensive, or his shield arm would give out and he'd be defenseless. He heard Kichu grunting as he hammered with his twin axes, telling him he couldn't expect any help from his Nephilim companion any time soon.

Japheth saw a second sappara lying on the ground near his feet and made a snap decision. He bull-rushed the pair, swinging like a madman, causing them to back up under the sudden and unexpected onslaught. Japheth used the momentary reprieve to drop his shield and scoop up the sappara. With two blades in his hands, Japheth felt more confident. He feinted left, drawing one of the Nephilim forward. Now they were split, and Japheth darted between them, hacking with the bladed outside edge at one Nephilim and hooking the heel of the second with the dull inside edge of his other weapon.

They both staggered and turned around to face him, but Japheth was already swinging, laying open a bare belly; Nephilim scorned any kind of armor, preferring to live or die by their martial skill. The other warrior, the largest one, charged Japheth, and he was forced to backpedal yet again, abandoning his attack.

The remaining Nephilim warrior was armed with a single axe nearly as long as Japheth was tall, and the enormous warrior was swinging it one-handed, as if it were a child's toy. Japheth had no intention of trying to block a blow from the weapon; if he tried, it would plow through his sword and cleave him in half without slowing—his only hope was speed.

Unfortunately, the Nephilim warrior, though nearly ten feet tall and built like an aurochs, was not the powerful-but-slow kind. He was quick and agile, and nearly lopped Japheth's head off before he had chance to so much as take a breath. He threw himself backward into the dirt, landing with such force that the wind was knocked out of him. Seeing stars and gasping for breath, Japheth rolled to the side to avoid the blade as it crashed into the earth next to him. Still trying to catch his wind, Japheth swept one sappara at the giant warrior's heel and yanked with all his might. He barely moved the hulk's leg. Laughter boomed out from above him, and Japheth saw the axe descending, as inevitable as sunset.

Kichu's smaller battleaxe intercepted the larger weapon, inches from Japheth's skull. He rolled away immediately, more than willing to let Kichu handle the behemoth. As he found his feet, however-er, Japheth noted that Kichu's left arm was curled against his side, bleeding from a gash along the bi-cep, so deep that bone showed white between rag-ged flesh-ends. The other warrior was unwounded and barely sweating, though the blade of his axe was coated in blood and his torso was spattered with it.

Around him, the battle was already fading as Emmen-Utu's and Sin-Iddim's combined forces be-gan to overrun the warriors left behind to defend Uruk. Japheth glanced around to see that Kichu's battle was being watched by most of the surviving warriors. Japheth wanted to rush in and help Kichu, who was at a disadvantage in the battle, wounded and weak from blood loss, but he dare not—Kichu's honor as a warrior and prince depended on the out-come of this fight.

Kichu was fighting smart, ducking and weaving, avoiding rather than blocking, saving his strikes for a moment when he knew he could draw blood. He took a glancing blow to the thigh that staggered him, and the monster from Uruk grinned savage-ly, pressing his advantage. He bulled into Kichu and knocked the smaller warrior flying. Kichu rolled, dropping his remaining axe in the process. With a roar of triumph, the warrior stomped through the intervening space, axe descending for the killing blow.

Japheth didn't stop to consider his next action—honor be damned. Kichu had saved his life, now it was time to return the favor. Three running steps and a leap took Japheth airborne, a single sappara singing through the still air, the other dropped to focus his energy on making one blow count. The warrior never saw him coming.

His head dropped to the dirt, eyes still blinking for a few heartbeats. Japheth landed, twisting his ankle painfully. He felt the tendon snap and tumbled to the earth next to the gore-seeping head.

There was a brief, fraught silence, then a deafening roar from the armies circled to watch. Kichu was still tensed for the blow that never came. When he realized it wasn't coming, he scrambled to his feet, saw the headless body bleeding into the hot sand, saw Japheth gripping his ankle, crimson-stained sappara still gripped in his exhausted hand.

"You should've let me die, you stupid little bastard," Kichu growled.

"But I didn't," Japheth said past clenched teeth.

Now that the adrenaline was leaving his system, his myriad aches and pains were making themselves known. On the battlefield, a handful of warriors from the conquering army were stepping around piles of bodies, prodding corpses with sword tips. Those wounded who might recover were pulled aside, and those too far gone to be saved were put out of their misery. Women carrying jugs of water were making their way across the battlefield, offering drinks of water, and officers were issuing commands.

The battle was over; it had lasted maybe thirty minutes all told, and already vultures were circling in the sky overhead. The joint armies of Emmen-Utu and Sin-Iddim were storming into the city, knocking down the gates to plunder and loot, rape and pillage—considered payment for the troops, who were expected to take whatever they could carry out, be it goods, gold, slaves, or women.

Japheth wanted none of it.

He hadn't died in the battle, he'd survived, and judging from the reaction of those gathered around him, he'd killed an important person in Uruk.

"Who was that?" Japheth asked, kicking the head.

Kichu laughed. "Of course you wouldn't know. That was Amar, crown prince of Uruk. He was the only possible heir, and it is likely his father, the king, is either dead right now, or he will be very soon."

This meant that Sin-Iddim and Emmen-Utu had just ended the dynasty which had ruled over Uruk for centuries. It also meant there would be squabbling and bartering between the two kings over who would rule in Uruk, now that the throne was empty.

Japheth found that he didn't really care. Kichu

had declined to join the pillaging of Uruk as well, and so he and Japheth were still on the battlefield, sitting on the side of an overturned chariot, sharing a wineskin, watching as vultures winged overhead and hopped from body to body. There were other kinds of vultures as well, the human kind, those beggars who followed an army to battle and waited for the carnage to end so they could loot the bodies of the slain.

"What the in the name of all the gods are you doing here, Japheth?" Kichu asked. "And in Larsan armor, no less."

Japheth shrugged and said cryptically, "It's where fate has taken me."

Kichu glared, helping him to his feet. "Give me a straight answer, little man."

Japheth cursed, propping himself up on his sword. "You want a straight answer, Kichu? All right, then, here's an answer for you: I love your sister, but your demon-god of a father married her to the foulest pig who's ever lived. I joined the Larsan army hoping to get close enough to Sin-Iddim to put a spear through his fat belly. It may not have allowed me to win back Aresia, but at least she wouldn't have to suffer at the hands of that vile old demon."

Kichu rocked back on his heels, stunned. "I knew you and my sister were meeting frequently, but . . . love? You are a fool, Japheth."

Japheth struggled to keep his face free of emotion. "I don't know for sure, but I'm fairly certain she agreed to marry Sin-Iddim to save me from your father. If that is so, then I could not allow that to go unrecognized. I may not have much, but I have my honor."

Kichu nodded. "Sin-Iddim has been after her for years. He asked Father for her hand in marriage at least twenty times, and every time Aresia kicked up such a fuss that Father always gave over, for he knows very well what Sin-Iddim is like." Kichu swore. "So, she has feelings for you, eh? She wouldn't agree to marry Sin-Iddim for just anything."

Japheth felt for the pendant. "He hates humans, as you well know, and learning his only daughter had lain with one was more that he could tolerate." He hesitated a moment. "My father worships Elohim, and I was raised to worship Him as well, although I'm not sure what I believe any longer."

Kichu laughed, shaking his head. "You're a bigger fool, Japheth, than I first imagined. Why would you admit these things to me?"

"Because we each owe the other a dozen lives," Japheth said, "and you cannot deny that."

Kichu looked down at the bloody sand between his feet, knowing the human was right; after all, Japheth had just saved his life mere moments ago.

Japheth continued, "And because I don't think you share your father's hatred for Elohim or for humans. But I don't care what you think. Whether I live or die no longer means anything to me."

"No? Then why did you fight so hard today to stay alive?"

Japheth was wondering the same thing. He shrugged, saying, "Instinct, I guess. I may not care if I live, but it's not in me to roll over and die either, especially not at the hands of some godless Nephilim dog."

This explanation amused Kichu, for he shook with silent laughter. "You have lost your mind, talking to me like that. You're all right for a human, but don't think I won't split your ugly skull like a pomegranate if you keep up that talk." Kichu's features smoothed out, as he turned serious once more. "So what are you going to do now? There's plenty of women in there." He jerked a thumb at Uruk, smoke and screams emanating from the walled city.

"I don't want those women. I want Aresia."

Kichu shook his head, his eyes narrowing in anger. "She's not for you, Japheth," he snapped. "She is a princess, and a Nephilim. You are a commoner, and a human—it's impossible."

"I know what you say is true, Kichu." Japheth hobbled on his twisted foot, testing it. "I have no plan, I cannot forget her. I can't . . ." Japheth trailed off and slumped back to the ground, too exhausted to remain on his feet.

"I don't have any answers for you, Japheth. If it were me, I would stay as far away from Larsa as I could. There is nothing for you here. Go back to Bad-Tibira, or go back to your family."

Japheth nodded, knowing Kichu was right. This battle had shown him that, for all his bravado, he wasn't quite ready yet to throw his life away. He would begin again, somewhere, somehow.

Kichu hauled Japheth to his feet. "I'll buy you a few rounds, take you dicing. Time will do the rest."

Japheth could only nod again. Wine, gambling, whores, none of that mattered. Aresia might as well be a star twinkling in the sky for all that he could reach her.

# CHAPTER 6

## Sorrow

"'I am sorry I ever made them.'" Genesis 6:7
(NLT)

M<small>Y PRAYERS THAT MY HUSBAND WILL BE</small> killed in battle go unanswered. He returns to Larsa filled with the pride of someone who always gets what he wants.

He comes to my rooms nearly every night, and he behaves as if he were still on the battlefield. My thighs and womanhood are sore from him, but he will not relent. He is punishing me for murdering his child, and I take his punishment because, deep down, I know I deserve it. Even the child of a monster like Sin-Iddim deserves to live, but I could not stomach the thought of bearing his child. I simply could not do it.

Poor Mirra. She did as I asked, and she died for it, as she knew she would. I saw the knowledge of death in her eyes when she left. I don't know how Sin-Iddim knew Mirra gave me the herbs. For all I know, he has her killed simply out of sheer petulance, for letting me miscarry. I do not know, and I cannot care. She is dead, and no prayers of mine can bring her back.

I still think of Japheth. His face erupts in my dreams. His tender lips brush mine as I sleep, and then I wake to an empty room and an aching heart. Irkalla has given up trying to rouse me, or cheer me. Days turn into weeks, and then weeks into months, and I allow myself to grow lethargic. I do not allow the servants to dress me or paint my eyes with kohl. I eat little and drink wine until the room spins from morning till night.

Sin-Iddim is furious. He married me for my beauty, and I have stolen it from him. He comes to me, rages at me, hits me, kicks me, curses me. Madness gleams in his eyes, and I find satisfaction knowing I put it there.

Or make it worse, at least. I believe he has always been mad, and I have simply thrown oil onto the fire.

This cannot continue. I will die soon, and I will welcome the darkness.

I do not know how much time has passed.

Sin-Iddim still comes, but not every night, not even once a week now. Perhaps he satisfies himself with that poor boy. I do not know that either, and I do not care.

If I do not waste away and die of starvation, perhaps I can make the demon-king kill me.

I think perhaps that would be best—better to die quickly, end the suffering of my broken and empty heart.

Thoughts of Japheth swirl through my clouded, drunken, hunger-hazed head. I can feel him, out there somewhere. I thought he might be close once, long ago. I thought I felt him nearby, but then it passed and I could only tip the wineskin and drown the agony of his imagined nearness.

Now he is far away, and Irkalla sits in a chair near my bed, eyes red-rimmed from weeping for me, even though I plead with her not to mourn for me.

I think I will send her away, and prod Sin-Iddim into beating me. The pain will wake me from my stupor, and he will kill me, and I will be free.

I did not imagine anything could hurt this badly; this is worse than the miscarriage. Fool that I am, I underestimated the demon-king's taste for savagery.

He did not merely beat me—he tortured me.

I no longer call on Inanna, for she is silent, as she has always been, as she ever will be. She is a dead god; she is no god at all; she is naught but empty air.

*Elohim, help me.* I called on The One God, finally. Not as I did when Father threatened Japheth, but for myself. Not to spare me, but to answer me. To speak to me.

*If you are Lord of Heaven, as your followers claim, you will answer me. I am dying, Elohim. I am alone, and I am dying. Speak to me, Elohim. Speak to me.*

Blood runs from my nose, from my ears, from the cleft between my thighs, from a thousand cuts upon every inch of my body. He burns the soles of my feet with red-hot sword tips; I can smell my flesh burning, a sick smell nightmarishly like roasting meat.

He rapes me as I bleed, his pig-thing smeared with my effluvia. He laughs as I weep.

When I pass into unconsciousness from the pain, he waits until I regain my senses, and then he turns me onto my stomach and sodomizes me. He forces himself into my mouth, sour with excrement, and his seed burns my throat and chokes me.

I bite him, and that is when his fists descend like hammers on a blacksmith's forge. When he breaks his knuckles on my face and ribs, he uses his feet.

I wake again, and I curse the knowledge that I am still alive. My heart continues to beat still, albeit weakly.

I am on the floor of my chamber, lying in a foul puddle from the over-turned chamber pot, bleeding, soiling myself, vomiting blood and weeping. I have lost hope, and I believe I will not die, but only continue on like this, drowning in this sea of unbearable agony but never grant the peace of death.

All through this, Irkalla is made to sit by and watch, prevented from intervening, prevented from leaving. Only after the king leaves is she allowed to go to my side and offer me what little comfort she can.

And that is when I hear a voice so strong, so calm, so loving that I can only imagine it is the voice of Elohim.

It is not a voice like a person's, human or Nephilim. It is . . . I do not know what it is.

Mortal language is not equipped to express the sound. It is like thunder booming in my bones, like the rumble of mountains shifting in their seats. It is like all the music of the world heard at once, heard in my bones and in my blood—it is the song of angels whispering in my ears, speaking peace unto my soul. The Voice is the sweet smell of orchids in my nostrils, of jasmine in the evening, a candle blown out, coils of smoke smelling acrid and sweet in the new darkness.

The Voice of The One God is familiar and dulcet, as many-faceted as a diamond.

His Voice shines in my soul like a torch in the dank heavy black of a dungeon. His Voice dawns brilliant in the prison-chamber of my wrecked soul.

All the poetry I possess is not enough beauty to encapsulate the heaven of His Voice.

*"DAUGHTER, BE STILL."*

How can I be still, when all I am is death and pain and heartbreak? Where were you when that mad man was doing this to me? Where were you when Japheth was ripped away from me? Why did you allow this, if you are God? Does my pain glorify you, my Lord?

*"YOUR LOVE GLORIFIES ME. YOUR FORGIVENESS GLORIFIES ME. YOUR LIFE GLORIFIES ME."*

If I was not weeping before, I am now. I am sobbing, hysterical and uncontrollable. His voice tolls in my heart, reverberates in my soul. Love echoes in his words. Peace radiates from his presence. The pain does not lessen, but I know He is with me.

It is enough.

I wake as rough hands lift me up into strong arms. I moan in pain. A harsh male voice shushes me, but not unkindly.

I hear Irkalla's voice in my ear: "You must be silent, my queen. Please, be quiet, so we may escape."

"I am . . . no queen," I mumble.

Sin-Iddim is a demon, not a king; I am not his wife, and I am not a queen. But I have not the strength for so many words. Irkalla understands and does not answer.

Her words filter through my pain . . .

Escape? There is no escape from the mad demon-king. He will find me. He would hunt me down and finish what he started.

I sputter, trying to say this to Irkalla, but her hand is pressed firmly against my split lips, stifling the sound of my words.

I pass in and out of consciousness, but I am aware of being carried down steps, through echoing hallways and out into the night. My eyes are swollen nearly shut, but I can still make out the moon, round and pregnant with silver light, illuminating countless stars in an endless arc across the sky. I smell night air, feel the cool breeze on my feverish forehead.

I am carried on a crude litter through the city, each step sending throbbing pain lancing through me. I moan, unable to stop the sound from escaping. Irkalla begs me to keep quiet, and I bite my tongue to still it.

Eventually, we approach the city gate. The man carrying me stops and curses, and Irkalla echoes his epithet.

"He is not supposed to be here," Irkalla mutters.

"Well, he is," says one of the men carrying me. "What do we do now?"

"I don't know, Uresh. Gods above, I don't know." Irkalla sounds near to weeping. "Marika promised me he'd be gone for an hour tonight, at this time."

The gate captain notices our approach, and he challenges us. I feel his bulk hovering close, staring down at me like a devouring presence. Fear seeps through my pores and into my blood; he is going to take me back to the demon-king.

I sob through cracked lips.

"Where are you taking her, servant girl?" The gate captain's voice sounds like rocks tumbling down a hill.

"Away. To be healed." Irkalla's voice is tense and small.

Silence, then: "This is the queen, is it not?" Irkalla doesn' answer, and the gate captain answers his own question. "It is she. I am not stupid, girl.

Did you think to deceive me?"

"No sir."

"Then tell me what you plan to do with her, and tell me why I shouldn't report you."

Irkalla doesn't answer, and I feel the danger increase. Then she speaks, finally, whispering. "I told you truly, sir. She is near death. I want to take her away to be healed. The king . . . he . . . he did this. She doesn't deserve this—no one does."

"That is not for you to decide. You should take her back before her absence is discovered. I am doing you a favor, just by telling you this much. I should march you back to the palace right now. It's my head if I'm discovered complicit in the escape of the queen."

He must have clamped a hand on her arm, for Irkalla whimpers in pain. "Please, *please*—don't."

"Why not? What's in it for me?" His voice is thick and suggestive.

I want to protest, tell Irkalla no, don't do that, not for me. But a calloused hand presses against my mouth, and I fall silent.

"Will you let us go?" Irkalla demands, her voice stronger. "Will you keep silent when the questions are asked?"

"Depends on how well you . . . *convince* me." I hear the leer in his voice, and know his price as well as Irkalla does.

Irkalla is a lovely girl, tall and buxom, fair-skinned and delicate. Men of all ranks have begged me for her hand, but I have refused them all. She had a lover, once, but he died on the battlefield and she would take no other . . . years passed and she kept her chastity.

And now, for me, she surrenders it to a hulking brute with hard hands.

I hear it all and I weep for her. I hear him grunting in pleasure as he drives himself into her. I am forced to listen to her whimpering, trying to sound encouraging. He is hurting her, I can tell; I hear it in her voice, for the sound of pain during sex is unmistakable.

The slap of flesh against flesh echoes loudly in the silent street.

It seems to last for an eternity, and through it all Irkalla tries to be . . . *convincing*. I crane my neck weakly, and I see her legs around his waist, her face turns to the side, tears leaking into the dust beneath her.

Finally, he finishes, and he leaves her lying in the dirt, her skirt still shoved up past her belly.

"You were convincing enough," he says. "You may go."

"Will you keep silent?" Irkalla's voice is calm, strong, and quiet.

"Yes, girl. You've bought my silence," the gate

captain growls. "Now go, before I change my mind and keep you for myself."

The road is long, silent, and rough. At least out on the open road my cries of torment—physical, mental, and emotional—will not bring ruin down upon us.

I do not cry out to Elohim or Innana. I cry out to no one but the silent stars and watching moon, and to Irkalla limping next to me, sniffling, her tears running freely.

An onager and a wagon waits for us some distance from the walls of Larsa. I am settled into the wagon and covered with a blanket. Irkalla thanks the guards then climbs in next to me. Only one of them accompanies us, a gruff, taciturn, hard-bitten man, the one Irkalla had named Uresh.

Uresh clucks his tongue, his shoulders hunch as if the weight of what he has seen is too heavy even for him to bear.

# CHAPTER 7

## Dust to Dust

'"By the sweat of your face you shall eat bread,
till you return to the ground, for out of it you
were taken; for you are dust, and to dust you
shall return."' Genesis 3:19 ESV

JAPHETH REMAINED IN URUK WITH THE
conquering armies for a few days, helping with
the mop-up efforts and patrolling to restore order
after the battle. And then, once some agreement
had been reached between the kings regarding the
fate of Uruk, the human mercenaries were paid and
dismissed; thus Japheth found himself wandering
back to Bad-Tibira in the company of a few other
mercenaries, his coin purse heavy and his heart
empty. He found a room to let, once again near the
wall where rent was cheap and questions few. It was

a risk returning to Bad-Tibira, he knew, but it as long as he laid low and didn't attract the attention of the king, his presence in the city would likely remain unnoticed.

He wasn't even sure why he'd returned, truth be told. It was home, or as near to one as he had; it was familiar, if nothing else.

He drank himself into a stupor at night, drinking until sleep claimed him. Sleep, however, didn't stop him from dreaming of Aresia. He saw her face in his dreams, saw her broken, bloody body in nightmares, ravaged by Sin-Iddim.

Then, the dreams began recurring. He saw her with a handmaiden and a single human guard, traveling an empty road, stopping in dank, smoke-fogged inns.

He felt her presence. Every passing day brought her closer. The idea was lodged in his fevered, drunken mind until he was more than half-mad with it. She was coming, somehow.

Two weeks after the battle against Uruk, the sense of Aresia's nearness was so strong as to drive him to restless pacing. He refused to sleep, pacing the road in front of Bad-Tibira's gates. His eyes were locked on the road, the gate, pacing restlessly, tirelessly back and forth in front of the gate, until the guards thought him mad. And, in truth, he felt mad but couldn't bring himself to care, so strong was the sense of Aresia's presence.

*Elohim,* he prayed finally, *if you bring her to me, I will turn away from the wine and the battlefield. I will serve you, Elohim, only bring her to me.*

He heard no voice, but he felt a peace in his soul, a quiet reassurance. He emptied his last wineskin in the dust at his feet, filled his belly with bread and meat until the dizziness abated, and prayed the prayer again and again. Hours passed—night fell, and day came, and then the noon sun beat down on him, rivulets of sweat pouring down his face and back, and still he waited, praying to Elohim, a single word chanted to the rhythm of his pacing feet: *please . . . please . . . please.*

Then the crunch of wagon wheels filled the air, and the braying of an onager brought Japheth to his feet. He watched with a thudding heart as the wagon drew nearer. Heat waves shuddered and wavered in the air, obscuring the occupants until they were within a bowshot. The driver was a middle-aged Nephilim man, bearded, grizzled, heavy-shouldered. He turned in the seat and spoke to one of the two smaller, hooded figures in the back of the wagon. One of them raised a head to peer at Japheth, nodded, and slumped back down.

He dared not hope, dared not think it was really happening. It was impossible.

The wagon drew up next to him, and the driver

spoke: "Are you Japheth, son of Noah?" Japheth nodded his assent. "Thank the gods we found you. Help me bring her in. She's weak."

"She?" Japheth couldn't allow his mind, his heart, to believe.

"Yes, *she*," the driver snapped. "I dare not speak her name, not here. Just bring her in, you fool."

Japheth circled to the back of the wagon and peered into the drawn hoods of the two robed figures seated there. One was a young woman, vacant brown eyes staring into space, sweat-damp mouse-brown hair sticking to her fair cheeks. Japheth knew her—she was Irkalla, the servant of Aresia. Her expression was haunted, traumatized, that of a woman who had known the rape of a conquering warrior; he'd seen the expression often enough to know it.

The other figure, leaning against the servant girl . . . Japheth held his breath as he stepped closer.

Aresia.

Japheth wept. Her lovely face was swollen, her nose broken and reset, her eyes black and blue and green and fading yellow. Her knees were drawn up beneath her, and she shivered, sweating. He saw the sole of a foot peeking out from beneath the folds of her robe; wide triangular brands were seared into the tender skin, overlapping and scattered in random patterns, the painful brands too numerous to count.

Japheth touched her cheek with a feather-light finger, and Aresia started, whimpered, and curled away into the servant girl.

"Shh, it's me," Japheth whispered. "It's Japheth. You're safe now. It's me. Open your eyes—you're safe."

Aresia cracked an eye open, hesitant and disbelieving. When she saw Japheth, she wept, cried out, and reached for him. Japheth caught her, lifted her up, and kissed her cracked, swollen lips. She was thin and frail, weak, so light now he could lift her without effort.

"Is it really you?" Aresia's voice was a hoarse whisper, her golden eyes peering into Japheth's, glittering with hope and fear. "Is it you? Are you real? Elohim, please. Don't mock me, thus."

"It's me—it's me." Japheth touched his lips to her forehead. "Elohim has brought you to me."

Aresia lifted a hand, touched his face, his mouth, his cheekbones, smiling. Then she passed out, going limp in his arms.

Japheth and Uresh drove the wagon near to his room. He carried her up to his room over the candlemaker's shop and laid her on his pallet of blankets, covering her gently.

Then he went back out to find Uresh, trying to coax Irkalla out of the wagon. She wouldn't let him touch her, shrinking away from him, shaking her head, moaning and whimpering.

Japheth motioned Uresh, climbed up, leaned close and whispered to her. "You're safe now, Irkalla. You know me. No one else will harm you. Come inside, please. Come inside. I won't touch you, I promise."

The girl glanced at Japheth, her eyes finally focusing. She looked from him, to the city around her, the people shuffling by with loads to sell at market, supplies to cook dinner, water from the well. Eyes stared at her, at the guard, at Japheth, and back to her. Booted feet tramped in the distance, spearheads flashed in the sun.

"Come, girl, come inside," Japheth repeated, keeping his voice low and calm. "The king's guards are coming."

"Irkalla, please . . . you must come inside, now." Japheth reached for her, but she pulled her arm away.

She seemed to rouse herself then, waking up finally. She looked over Japheth's shoulder at the formation of city guards approaching, and fear crossed her features. She reached out, not for Japheth, but for Uresh. He too was glancing over his shoulder at the approaching soldiers, shifting his feet nervously. When Irkalla reached for him, he gathered her in his arms and lifted her down from the wagon bed, as Japheth had Aresia.

Japheth led the way back to his room. Uresh sat down in a corner, Irkalla still cradled in his arms. Japheth heard him muttering to her. "You are safe now, Irkalla. I will protect you. I won't let that ever happen again." His voice was soft, surprisingly gentle for so rough a man.

Japheth wondered at that, but dismissed it—Irkalla and the guard would have to wage their own wars. He checked to make sure Aresia was still sleeping, and then gathering his remaining coin he left, telling the Larsan to not let anyone in unless it was Japheth himself. The healer who'd tended to Japheth's foot lived near the market at the center of the city, and it was her he sought now. He found her grinding herbs with a mortar and pestle.

"Please, mistress, will you come?" Japheth asked. "I need you, please. I have coin." Japheth showed a flash of gold.

"What is it you need me for?" The healer was an old woman, granite-gray hair still thick, eyes sharp and clear, her fingers quick and strong.

"A girl . . . my woman, she's hurt."

"Well, I need to know more than that, boy. Hurt how? Is she with child? Has she bones broken? A fever? Courses won't stop? I can't bring the right herbs if I don't know what ails her."

"I don't know, woman! She's been . . . tortured, I think. Her feet were . . . branded. Her nose is broken, but it's been reset, I think." Japheth paused, running his hands through his hair in frustration. He didn't really know the extent of her injuries. "She's been abused, sexually—I'd gamble the king's own life on it. I think it's safe to assume that if harm can be done to a body, it's been done to her."

The healer gathered various pouches, sniffing some and replacing them, choosing others, muttering to herself. Finally, she nodded and gestured for Japheth to lead the way.

They made their way through the thronging city to Japheth's room near the wall. Uresh and Irkalla were asleep, Irkalla still in his arms. Aresia was awake now, lying on the pallet on the floor, watching the door with panic in her eyes as Japheth entered.

"You left, Japheth. I woke—and you—you . . . weren't here." She reached a trembling hand for him, unable to lift her arm more than a few inches off the bed, tears spilling from her eyes at the pain from simply breathing, simply lifting her hands.

"I have a healer. I'm here now, I'm back." Japheth knelt beside her, taking her hands in his. "Can you tell her how you're hurt?"

"Everything," Aresia whispered. "He . . . he hurt . . . everything."

The healer knelt on the floor beside Aresia, pulled the blankets aside, and then had Japheth help remove Aresia's clothes so she could examine her more thoroughly. Anger boiled hot and hard through Japheth at the mass of bruises covering Aresia's body; fingerprints dotted her upper arms, her stomach and ribs were a solid mass of bruises in various states of progression, some older and yellowing, others fresh and angry blue-black. By the time she was undressed, Aresia had passed out once again from the pain.

The healer tsked and clucked her tongue, shaking her head, sinking back on her heels. "This poor girl has been beaten badly. I don't think she has a single rib intact. It's a miracle she's alive. Elo—I mean . . . Innana has shown her favor."

Japheth caught the slip. "It's okay, mistress—you may call on Elohim without fear."

The healer turned her piercing blue eyes on Japheth, searching for deception. "You did this to her?"

"No! I swear on my life, I swear on the name Elohim, The One God. I did not do this. I love her."

The healer nodded, accepting Japheth's word at face value, and turned back to Aresia. "She is no commoner. Her skin is too fine and well cared for beneath the bruises. Her fingers are too soft to have known work. Who is she?"

Japheth saw no reason to lie. "She is Aresia, daughter of Emmen-Utu, and wife of Sin-Iddim, king of Larsa."

"God above, boy! What is she doing here? And in such a state? You'll get us all killed!"

"Not if no one speaks of this. The only ones who know she is here are those two, and they will not speak. The other girl may need your attention as well. She has the look of one who has been raped."

"Unless she's bleeding, there's little I can do for that. She'll either move on, or she'll never be the same. It's the lot of a woman, in this life."

"It should not be."

The healer looked hard at Japheth. "You're a warrior. You mean to tell me you've never looted a city? You've never taken the spoils of war?"

"I've killed in battle, and I've looted my share of goods, but I've never raped a woman. I take no pleasure in the pain of a woman."

As she conversed with Japheth, the healer was wrapping rags around Aresia's torso, binding her broken ribs with poultices to reduce the swelling. When the healer began to examine Aresia's womanhood, Japheth turned away and stared out the window, trying in vain to push down the rage boiling in his gut.

"You love her," the healer remarked.

Japheth could only nod, still looking out the window.

"She will recover," the healer said. "Elohim has spared her life. I would not have expected her to live, if I had seen her but a few days ago. She is a strong young woman. But . . . I would not expect her to want to lay with you any time soon. She has been through much suffering."

"I know. I wouldn't—I mean . . . no. She is alive, and she is with me. That is enough."

The healer rose and stood next to Japheth at the window, touched his arm and met his gaze. "There is more. She may not wish you to know this, but I think you should. She has lost a child in the recent past. Her womb is still tender, still slightly hard to the touch, as of a woman who has been pregnant. I suspect she may have used certain herbs to cause this to happen."

Japheth buried his face in his hands, stifling a shuddering groan. "She was with child? It was *his* child then. It would not surprise me if she took something to rid herself of a child fathered by that monster."

"You speak of Sin-Iddim?"

"Yes. He is a demon."

"I have heard stories of him. His brutality is legendary, even here. I tended a boy once, who had served in Sin-Iddim's court. He spoke of sodomy."

"Yes. It is common in his court, from what I know."

The healer's voice was pitched low now, hesitant. "She has suffered this as well, I am afraid. I'm sorry."

"I wish I could say I was surprised." Japheth handed the old woman a coin. "Thank you. Is there anything I should do to care for her?"

"Willow bark, boiled as tea; it will help the pain. I have some I can give you. Send for me in a few days, and I will change the dressing on her ribs." She shrugged and pocketed the coin. "Everything else is only a matter of time. See that she eats and drinks, let her rest, and do not upset her. Just . . . give her your love, patience, and understanding, and Elohim will see to the rest. Pray."

"Thank you again. I will send my Larsan friend there to fetch you in a few days' time."

The first hours after the healer's departure were the hardest. Japheth's room was silent but for the soft breathing of three sleeping people. He was alone with his thoughts, his fears and worries. He had the daughter of the king—and the wife of another king—in his house. She was a fugitive. Sin-Iddim would be looking for her, and he would at the very least send a messenger to Emmen-Utu. The city would be searched.

They must leave. They couldn't stay in Bad-Tibira, that much was clear; Aresia, however, was simply too badly hurt to be moved. She needed rest, and to be near a healer Japheth could trust.

A burst of panic assaulted him—he couldn't care for a woman; he didn't know how. Where could he go? The only trade he knew was war, and that meant leaving Aresia's side for days and weeks at a time, and eventually he would die in battle, and she would be left alone. He couldn't risk that. She was helpless on her own . . . she'd never known the day-to-day hardships of life. However difficult her father may have been, she was still a princess, pampered, and she had grown up with every physical comfort. Now, after her time in the clutches of Sin-Iddim, she was badly injured only just this side of Death's door. He couldn't leave her to go and find mercenary work; she would wake up and need him.

Japheth paced the room, hunger gnawing at him, but fear of her waking up alone kept him in the house. The guard was still asleep as well, clearly exhausted from their flight from Larsa, as was the servant girl, Irkalla.

A single thought entered his head, and he stopped pacing, turning the idea over in his mind.

Noah.

Japheth hadn't seen his father or mother in years. It would gall his pride, but they might take him back in, help him see to Aresia's care until she was healed. After three children, his mother knew enough of herbs and poultices and such, and his father could always use the extra help on the farm, which was remote, far removed from any city and the risk of discovery. The thought of crawling back to Noah made Japheth's gut writhe and burn in anger, but it was the only viable option left.

He'd have to apologize, and his father would demand his obedience.

And then there was the problem of Neses; the girl he had been betrothed to when he was just a boy. Noah and the girl's father, Namus, had made the match while Japheth and Neses were both still children, but Japheth had refused to comply. When he was old enough he had run away to join King Emmen-Utu's army before the marriage could be arranged.

He had no idea what had happened to Neses in the intervening years . . . she was a nice enough girl, and pretty, but he had refused to marry someone simply because his father said so. If Japheth went back, would Noah and Namus try to force the marriage again?

That was a risk he'd have to take, for Aresia's sake. She needed considerable care, and she couldn't go back to her old life. Not now.

Japheth was reminded of the promise he'd made: he owed Elohim worship in exchange for Aresia's life . . . and his own life too, perhaps.

Evening sunlight streamed in through the

window, bathing the room with a golden square. His home was a simple one, a single room located near the city wall, near the gate, overlooking the city. Japheth stood, leaning his shoulder against the doorway, watching the foot and cart traffic in the road below, hearing the bray of onagers and the bellow of oxen, the yell of drivers.

He'd called Bad-Tibira home for so long now that the thought of his father's farm seemed alien and distant. He'd been so young when he left, so idealistic and hard-headed. His father had been worse, unmoving in his morals, harsh in the demands he'd made of his eldest son. The rift between them had been inevitable, it seemed to Japheth, looking back. He was so much like Noah in so many ways that two such men under one roof was all but impossible.

Japheth tried to imagine returning to his father's farm, but he simply couldn't picture it.

He turned to watch Aresia as she slept, her battered but lovely features slack and at peace; could he make amends with his father, for her sake?

He turned back to watch the sun drop below the city wall. *Elohim, guide me*, Japheth prayed. It felt strange to pray now, after so long, but he did it anyway. Elohim was the only god he could put any stock in, having spent his entire adult life watching the futile, brutal, empty worship the Nephilim gave their gods.

He had little choice, it seemed . . .

He would return, after many years, to his father's home.

Immediately, he set about formulating plans and gathering the necessary supplies for the three-day journey. Japheth tried to tell himself he wasn't nervous.

But it didn't work.

He would rather have gone into battle naked and unarmed than have to ask his father to take him in.

# CHAPTER 8

## Noah

"Noah was a righteous man, blameless in his
generation." Genesis 6:9 ESV

SUNLIGHT ON MY FACE—AS BRIGHT AND HOT AS
the pain in my bones—woke me. Consciousness
was immediately accompanied by a thousand aches,
pangs of pain in every joint, in every muscle. Then
came the realization that I was moving. I felt the
slow sway and jounce of a wagon across a pitted
road. I heard the *hee-haw* of onagers, and the sound
of hooves on hard-packed dirt. I lay quietly, trying
to imagine where I was.

I caught myself on the verge of swearing by
Inanna, but stopped myself: I no longer believe in
her, and haven't for a long time, but wanted to swear
by her out of life-long habit.

By whom do I swear, now?

It felt blasphemous to swear by the name of The One God, wrong in a way it never did to curse by Inanna or Ereshkigal. Elohim is real, I think, and to use his name for so vulgar a thing as cursing seems wrong. But yet . . . the way I feel at this moment warrants a curse of some kind.

I contented myself with a groan and a curse I've heard from soldiers: "Shit."

A hand touched my cheek, knuckles brushing my forehead. "You're awake." Japheth's voice washed over me, familiar and welcome.

I had worried, upon waking, that this had all been a dream that I would wake from back in Sin-Iddim's palace or on the road.

"Yes, I am awake," I croaked. "Unfortunately."

"How do you feel?" Japheth asked.

"Not good," I answered. "Beaten, raped, and broken."

Silence fell for several moments.

"You're safe now," Japheth said. "No one will ever hurt you again, I promise."

I wished I could believe him, but I didn't.

I tried to force myself to a sitting position, and the effort left me sweating, cursing in pain—I gave up before I passed out, and settled into a slightly more elevated position, enough that I could rest my head against the wall of the wagon bed, my ribs screaming agony, every breath an agony.

"Where are we going?" I gasped, when the pain had receded enough to allow me speech.

We were alone on the road, and I was alone in the wagon, facing Japheth's back as he sat on the bench, driving the onagers. It was a small thing, a two-wheeled cart pulled by a pair of onagers, their round, powerful, tawny bodies drawing the cart effortlessly, knobby knees seeming too small for their fat bodies, long dark tails swishing at flies.

The land around us was flat in every direction, plowed and furrowed in wide squares of verdant green, broken by river channels and undeveloped swaths of swampland, all divided by this road on which we traveled, a high-banked, hard-packed line of dirt through the countryside.

Japheth did not answer for such a long time I began to wonder if he had heard me.

"Japheth?" I stared at his broad, hunched back. "Answer me—where are we going? Where are Irkalla and Uresh?"

"We're going to my father's house," Japheth said, eventually, his voice heavy. "Irkalla and Uresh are still in Bad-Tibira; they are staying in my room for now. Uresh said he has family in Kutallu, so they will go there, eventually. Once Irkalla is well enough to travel."

A thousand questions were banging through

my mind. "Why did she not come with us? She is my maidservant . . . I have not gone anywhere without her since I was a little girl. What is happening, Japheth?" The questions took every bit of strength I had.

"She is not sick in her body, not in a way any healer could fix," Japheth replied. "She is sick in her mind, in her soul. Whatever it was she endured has damaged her. Uresh cares for her—he will see her well, if she has the courage to let herself be well again." Japheth turned in the wagon seat and looked at me. "I told you, we're going to my father's house. You will be safe there. He lives far from anyone."

"Why?" My mind was not working properly. I could not understand why we would go to Noah's home.

"Think, Princess: you ran away from Sin-iddim, and he will not let that go. He will send soldiers to Bad-Tibira to search for you, and if your father knows where you are, he will hand you straight back to that monster. In any of the cities in Sumer you are known, so we risk discovery anywhere we might go.

"I do not know any other trade besides war, and I haven't enough money to support us without finding work. I cannot leave you alone long enough to escort some fat nobleman from one place to another. Besides which, you are injured. It will be months before you're well enough to even walk on your own, much less learn to survive alone in a city while I'm gone." He shook his head and sighed. "No, Princess, the only place we have a chance to see you well again is my father's farm."

A bolt of anger seared through me. "Stop calling me that."

"Stop calling you what?" Japheth twisted on the bench and shot me a quizzical look.

"Princess—I am not a princess anymore, and I am most certainly not a queen. I am just . . . Aresia."

"Aresia, then," Japheth said, reaching behind himself and squeezing my ankle.

I found a measure of comfort in his touch, but something was bothering him—I could feel it radiating off of him in palpable waves.

"What is wrong, Japheth?" I asked.

"Nothing."

I did not believe him, not for a second. "Do not lie to me—I am not blind."

Japheth clicked his tongue and snapped the reins to get the onagers moving more quickly as we hit an upward incline, and once again he was silent so long I thought he wasn't going to answer me.

He chuckled mirthlessly, and then sobered again. "It's my father . . . I've never gotten along with him very well. I left home when I was young. I was still a boy, really, but I was sick of his rigid morality, his unbending devotion to Elohim . . . everyone else had to believe the way he did, everyone had to live the way he commanded, and his word was law, no matter what. I could not live with him, so I left."

More silence, and then he continued.

"Looking back I realize the problem is, we are very much alike, my father and I. We argued all the time, and neither one of us would bend. I'm the same way, even still. More so, now that I'm a grown man. Then I was rebellious because that's just how children are, and it's still true now—I just can't make myself give in to anyone. It's what got us into this trouble in the first place. If I had been sensible about things, in the very beginning, I would've left Bad-Tibira, I would've forgotten about you and moved on. You would've found a decent husband among the Nephilim. You would never have agreed to marry Sin-Iddim if it hadn't been for me."

I shook my head, unable to find a response to his words.

"Japheth . . . it is not your fault," I said. "Not . . . not entirely. It is mine too. I wanted you, and I would not allow anyone to deny me. I knew seeing you was dangerous. If not for me, you would never have come to my father's attention. So . . . the fault is mine as much as it yours."

Japheth sighed, scrubbing his face with his hands. "It doesn't matter whose fault it is. We must walk the path set before us."

His words saddened me, and he seemed re-signed. Silence settled over us for many miles, both of us lost in our thoughts. The day dragged on, and the miles passed behind us, and I slept as much as I could. Japheth passed me a wineskin and meal-cakes, the kind of provision a soldier carries with him on marches to battlefields, wheat and barley packed into small discs and baked with honey. They were crunchy and filling and slightly sweet, but difficult to eat.

Night drew down upon us and Japheth finally pulled the wagon off the road into a turn-off that seemed to be designed for this purpose. There was ring of stones around a deep pit, filled with charred hunks of palm wood and ash, and a small pile of logs near the fire.

Japheth left me in the wagon bed and knelt beside the fire pit, stirring the ashes to find a bed of dull orange coals. Blowing on the embers and slowly adding bits of kindling, the flames flickered to life. He added a few larger sticks and then, as the fire grew, he added a single full-sized log. Returning to the wagon, Japheth slid his arms around me and effortlessly lifted me from the wagon, setting me on the ground near the wagon wheel, my feet facing the fire. The onagers were freed from their harness and staked to the ground a few feet away, bags of grain tied around their noses.

Then he dug in a basket in the back of the wagon and produced several jars of salves and herbs, as well as some food. The salve he put on my injuries, and the herbs he ground up and mixed with some water from a jug, which he then heated over the fire and bade me drink. The food was simple, some dried meat, a mix of dried fruit and nuts, and some hardened bread. Nothing fancy, but enough to fill our bellies.

After seeing to the animals and stirring the fire, Japheth finally stretched out on the ground next to me, piling his cloak beneath his head. I watched him fall asleep, his breathing evening out almost as soon as he closed his eyes; it took a lot longer for me to finally fall asleep.

I stared up at the silver wash of stars and the waning moon; palm trees waved their broad leaves in the soft breeze, a tiny stream nearby trickled in the distance, which I realized must be an offshoot of the Euphrates. It was peaceful, here, so far away from Larsa and Bad-Tibira, away from Father and Sin-Iddim and the palace and soldiers . . . it wasn't silent—the night was filled with trilling toads and croaking frogs, chirruping crickets, night birds winging above my head, black shapes against the stars flitting in pursuit of insects—but it was peaceful.

I thought of Irkalla and all she had done for me,

what she had suffered for me. *Elohim, be with her,* I prayed. I hated that I could do nothing to repay her, that I could not even thank her.

Absent was the threat of men seeking me, as well as the fear of my father's temper and the fear of Sin-Iddim's cruel hands. The thought of my erstwhile husband sent shivers down my spine; I wanted to believe I would be safe with Japheth at his father's home. Fear won out, however . . . Sin-Iddim would not rest until I was found. He would, as Japheth said, send soldiers to Bad-Tibira. Might he go so far as to scour the countryside? It seemed unlikely; there was simply too much area to cover. More likely, Sin-Iddim would accuse Father of going back on his word, of spiriting me away.

Would there be war between the cities once more, this time over me? They were proud, cruel men, my father and Sin-Iddim.

I realized something, lying there beneath the stars: no matter what the future held, I did not possess the courage to return to my old life, even if it did mean war between Larsa and Bad-Tibira.

We left the camp at dawn. With every mile that passed, Japheth grew ever more tense. I watched his shoulders tighten, watched the corners of his eyes narrow, and noticed his fingers clench white around the reins.

I tried to reassure him, but he refused to respond, only shaking his head, black curls bouncing against his forehead. At length I fell silent and allowed him to brood in peace.

Something had changed in Japheth, I realized. He was different. Gone was the brash, confident, arrogant man I'd been swept up by. This Japheth was sour, curt, introspective. I didn't like him much, but what could I do? I didn't know how to draw him out of his shell, what questions to ask. Indeed, I myself had changed, and I knew it. I had no desire to speak of what I'd endured, I only wanted to forget, to put time between me and the memories; perhaps Japheth was going through a similar process of trying to forget. Whatever the case, Japheth spoke little as we traveled, and if his sour silence hurt, I also understood it, for I had little to say myself.

Boredom set in quickly as league after league, hour after hour, passed in total silence.

We turned off the main road near sundown, breaking away to head due west. The smaller side road was narrow and very rugged, sending lances of pain through me at every turn of the wheels. I ground my teeth against it for as long as I could, but eventually a cry broke loose, and then I could no longer contain the whimpers.

The sound of my tears brought Japheth up from his torpor, and he turned to glance at me with concern.

"It is not far now. The farm is just over that rise," he said, pointing ahead.

I lifted up, gasping at the effort, to look ahead. The land drew itself up into a steep hill, cutting off our view of the land beyond the horizon. I settled back down and closed my eyes, willing the throb of my knitting bones to ease. After a while I felt the wagon tilt as we began the upward journey. Japheth called encouragement to the onagers as they struggled with the steep upward grade. I felt myself sliding downward, gripping the sides of the wagon to hold myself in place.

It should have been a simple thing, holding myself in place as we traveled up the hill, but it took every shred of my strength. I pinched my eyes shut, my teeth grating at the effort, my heart pounding.

At long last the hill leveled out and the wagon pulled to a stop. I heard Japheth climb out of the wagon and whisper praise to the onagers.

Then I heard a soft curse of surprise from him, followed by a word breathed in awe.

I struggled to turn around, but couldn't. I was slumped against the back of the wagon, fighting tears of pain.

"Japheth? What . . . what is it?" I managed.

He didn't answer. He simply turned and lifted me from wagon, holding me in his arms to show me the view of his father's farm.

What I saw took my breath away.

What I saw appeared to be a boat of some kind, massive enough to plow the starry waves of the very heavens. It was a skeleton only, a spare shape of struts and spars and curving ribs, but the scope of it, the size of it even from this distance of many miles was enough to stun me into breathless silence.

We stared for many minutes, awed.

"What in all the names of God is my father building?" Japheth whispered, more to himself than to me.

# CHAPTER 9

## Favor Found

"But Noah found favor with the Lord." Genesis
6:8

NOAH, SON OF LAMECH, SON OF METHUSELAH, was a frightening man. His beard was long and black, shot with streaks of gray, the tip brushing his belly. His curly black hair, so like Japheth's but long and unkempt, was tossed in the ever-present breeze, brushing across his eyes as he stood before the mountain-sized construction, a mallet in one hand and a thick, gnarled staff in the other. He wore a short knee-length, sleeveless tunic belted with a thick strap of leather. He was burly and tall, towering nearly half a cubit above Japheth, his shoulders as wide and heavy as an ox's, his arms thick and hairy, his chest as broad and round as a barrel of wine;

he could wrestle an aurochs and win. Noah was an imposing man, even to me, a Nephilim. His eyes were as blue as Japheth's but immeasurably older and sparking with wisdom. They pierced me like hurled spears.

He did not have to speak a word for me to know he hated me.

I could see this even as we approached. I sat next to Japheth in the wagon's seat, holding myself erect through sheer force of will. Noah's eyes narrowed as we neared him, until they were slits of blue that flashed with sparks. I refused to cower underneath his gaze, but I wanted to. Even Japheth kept rolling his shoulders back and straightening his spine, as if he too felt the weight of Noah's disapproval.

"Your father is . . . fearsome," I whispered, as we approached.

Japheth sighed. "Yes," he agreed.

Japheth's mouth was pressed into a thin line. I was quickly realizing the enmity between him and his father went deeper than he had let on. He wasn't merely tense—he was afraid. I had seen him face my father's men without blinking, and I had seen him kill men without so much as flinching, and he prophesied my father's death without fear, but now, at the prospect of seeing his own father, Japheth seemed to be nothing so much as terrified.

Japheth tugged on the reins and the onagers

slowed to a stop in front of Noah. Two other men stood behind Noah, one with a stack of planed and sanded boards in his arms, the other with a bucket of pitch. Both of these men shared Noah's black curls and blue eyes, making them Japheth's brothers, I assumed. They paused mid-motion as we approached, shock on their faces.

Stepping down from the wagon, Japheth squared his shoulders and faced his father; neither man spoke for long, tense minutes.

"Father," Japheth began. "It's been . . . a long time."

Noah remained silent, twisting the staff in his fist so the tip dug into the grass. "Japheth."

It was odd, Noah's greeting. It was not a welcome, not a greeting, and not a question. It seemed like nothing so much as an empty statement, a bare, spare acknowledgement of his son's presence.

"I . . . I know there's much we have to discuss, and I don't expect an eager welcome, but . . ." Japheth trailed off, ducking his head and toying with the ear of the onager munching grass next to him. "I hope . . . I was hoping we can . . . stay here, for at least a few days. Aresia, she's hurt . . . she needs time to recuperate."

Noah's jaw worked slowly, grinding his jaws together, and his eyes fixed on me, his upper lip curling. "You bring a Nephilim *here*? To *my* home?

Who is she? Why have you returned after so long?" Noah's words came in a flood, his voice deep and booming and rough.

Japheth looked back at me, and then to his father, as if wondering what to tell him, suddenly seeming at a loss. Japheth, so deadly and graceful and fearless on the battlefield, was afraid of his father.

I gathered my breath and my courage and stepped out of the wagon. I couldn't stop the gasp and whimper of pain as my ribs protested the movement. My legs wobbled, and I used the strong, broad backs of the onagers to support myself as I shuffled gingerly next to Japheth. He wrapped his arm around my waist and held me upright.

"I am Aresia, daughter of Emmen-Utu, King of Bad-Tibira," I said with all the strength I possessed, but it still came out breathless and soft.

Noah's face contorted in rage. "You bring to me the daughter of that—that godless savage? You sully my lands with the spawn of that *monster?* Have you gone mad, Japheth?" His voice shook, trembled.

"I know, Father. I know the enmity you harbor for Nephilim, but—"

"No, you foolish child. You don't know. You know nothing." Noah spat on the ground, a thick gobbet of saliva splatting into the dust. "Leave now. She is not welcome here and neither are you."

"Father, please—just listen to me. She's not like him . . . Aresia is not guilty of the sins of her father."

"She is a worshipper of the false gods." Noah turned away from his son. "And so are you, probably."

"No, Father. I . . . worship Elohim—I found Him, and I have returned to you. Please, Father," Japheth caught his father's sleeve, a simple act, but coming from a man so proud as Japheth, it was an abject plea. "Give us a chance."

I took a wobbling step, shaky as a newborn calf. "Please, Noah. We have nowhere else to go. I will tell you my story if you wish, but . . ." Noah stepped back from me, as if my mere proximity made him ill. "I do not worship my people's gods any longer. I—I have heard the voice of Elohim. He spoke to me—"

Noah lunged at me, spitting rage. "Do not blaspheme the name of The One God!"

He seemed about to strike me but wrenched himself away. His hatred was palpable and powerful, and I wondered what had happened to cause such ire.

"I speak the truth! I heard His voice. He . . . he spoke to me, when I was dying." I wavered on my feet, unable to stand any longer. Japheth caught me and lowered me to the ground.

Just then, an older woman approached, her

hair as black as her husband's and sons', but it was straight and fine, and her eyes were deep brown, kind and wide. She was beautiful, in the faded way of a woman who was once a glorious beauty and had aged well. She strode up to Japheth without pause and wrapped her arms around his neck, holding him close in a tight embrace. Japheth stood stiff for a moment, and then slowly relaxed, hands finally lifting to return the embrace. He held her for a moment and then attempted to pull away. The woman shook her head and pulled him back in. I heard her murmur something to him. Japheth shook his head, tried again to pull away, and the woman—his mother, obviously—held tight once more, her shoulders trembling.

I expected Japheth to push her away, but he didn't. He turned his face to the sky, as if beseeching his One God, and I saw a tear trembling in his eyes. He blinked hard, fighting the tears as his mother kissed him on his cheek, first the right and then the left. Then she took his face in her hands and kissed his forehead. Tears coursed down his cheeks.

"You came back. My son has returned." She rounded on Noah, eyes blazing. "How dare you turn him away, you stubborn old bull? He is our son, our eldest child. He has returned, and we will welcome him with open arms. Now, Japheth, who have you brought with you?"

I tried to rise to my feet but couldn't.

Japheth knelt down and lifted me up, holding me in his arms like a child.

"Mother, this is Aresia; Aresia, this is my mother, Zara."

Zara touched my blackened eyes with a gentle, practiced touch, ran her finger down the line of my broken nose, prodded my ribs. "Oh, child. Who did this to you?" The question was rhetorical, it seemed, for she continued speaking without giving me pause to answer. "Bring her into the house, Japheth. Ham, fetch me water and heat it. Shem, slaughter a sheep so we may feast your brother's return. Noah . . . you go away, and stay away until you can see fit to welcome your son properly. Speak to your God and learn forgiveness."

Shem and Ham both scurried to do their mother's bidding, but the glares they shot Japheth as he carried me toward the house suggested they, too, were not pleased about Japheth's return. They did not even bother to look at me.

The house was a long, low, squat structure built of stone and logs and mud-bricks, a thick plume of smoke rising from the center.

Within, I saw the organized chaos of a busy home. Zara had bustled ahead of Japheth and I, and was barking orders at three other, younger women, who vanished from the house to carry out Zara's commands.

The younger of Japheth's brothers—a hawk-nosed man with slim shoulders and a scar on his face pulling his lip into a perpetual sneer—brought two buckets of water on a yoke over his neck, staggering with the awkward gait of someone carrying a heavy load. He set them down by the fire pit at the center of the room, then set a huge copper pot on a stand above the fire and dumped the water in, and returned outside to fetch more. I heard a sheep bleating, a furious, panicked sound, and then silence. A few minutes later the older brother, Shem, came in with a bloody, skinned carcass and set it on a table. He pulled a long knife from a sheath at his side and set about carving the goat with practiced expertise, his hands red with the animal's blood.

Japheth had set me down near the fire, propping pillows behind me. He sat down beside me. "Don't worry, Aresia. Mother will set things right. Father will come around, eventually. I know he's a bit . . . intimidating . . . but he will calm down." And then, more to himself than to me, he muttered, "I hope."

"What does he have against my father?" I asked. "I know Father has a history of antagonizing your people, but your father seems to have something . . . personal."

Japheth looked puzzled. "I don't know. I know

he hates Nephilim, but this is . . . surprising, even to me."

Zara came over then, juggling pots of herbs and a swath of bandages. "Hush, children. Now is not the time to discuss old memories. Everything in its own time." She waved Japheth away. "Shoo, child. Help your brother carve the sheep. Better yet, go find your father and make amends. You hurt him deeply, leaving like you did, and the only way he can show his hurt is with anger—this you know, for you are much the same. He has a sensitive heart beneath all that bluff and bluster."

Japheth nodded, touched me on the forehead, and left the house.

I marveled at Zara. She spoke to Japheth as if he had been gone a matter of days, perhaps weeks, rather than years. She peeled away my robes, examining the bandages the healer had wrapped around me before we had left Bad-Tibira.

"Well, at least the healer knew what she was doing. Your ribs are well on their way to healing. Your nose, though. Whoever set that . . . well . . . we'll have to re-break it, I'm afraid. You're far too beautiful to have a crooked nose." Zara looked down at me, her brown eyes kind but strong. "Are you ready, child?"

She didn't wait for an answer. She reached up with calloused, powerful hands and gripped my nose between her palms, giving a hard jerk with one hand. Fire bolted through my face, a pain worse than when Sin-Iddim had broken it to begin with. I screamed, choking when blood sluiced down my throat.

"Almost done," Zara said. "This part will hurt as well. Ready?" Once again, she didn't give me a chance to respond.

She pressed her palms against my nose again and pulled out, away from my face, peering down at me critically before adjusting the set of my nose. I screamed past grinding teeth when the bones stretched apart, and then slid into place, guided by Zara's hands. Blood flooded from my nose, salty and hot and thick in my mouth, coating my chin and chest. She wiped my face clean with a rag, folded it, and then pressed it to my nose tenderly, pushing my hand up to hold it in place.

"There, now . . . it is done. I will look over the rest of you." Zara raised an eyebrow, not asking for permission.

Quick, gentle hands probed my belly, my thighs, slipped up to my womanhood, gently but thoroughly examining.

Knowing eyes met mine. "You've miscarried."

I nodded. "How can you tell?"

"You flinched at my touch, and your belly still seems to be healing. The flesh between your thighs shows evidence of having been . . . brutalized, and your other injuries all speak of a man's angry attention. Such a thing often leads to pregnancy. You are weak, weaker than you should be, even with such injuries, which means you must have lost a lot of blood not too long past. The herbs that cause miscarriage often lead to excessive bleeding."

"All true."

"Who was it that did this to you?"

I hesitated to answer. I wanted to trust this woman, but was not sure how far I could.

"Speak openly, child," Zara insisted. "You're safe here, I promise."

"Sin-Iddim."

Zara's hand jerked back from me. "The king of Larsa? Who *are* you, girl?

I realized she had been absent when I introduced myself to Noah. "My father is the king of Bad-Tibira."

Zara rubbed her forehead with a knuckle. "Oh, Japheth. What have you gotten yourself into?" This was muttered quietly, not addressed to me. "I see. Well, it's no wonder my husband reacted so strongly to your presence. So you ran from your husband, and somehow ended up with my son, who brought you here? I assume they will be looking for you?"

I was not ready to speak of what had happened to me, not yet. "There will be men looking for me, yes. I doubt they will know to come here, though. No one knew I was with Japheth, except my maidservant, and she would die rather than give me up."

Zara shook her head as she re-wrapped the bandages around my torso. "Well, we can only hope they don't come here. We'll have to keep watch, just in case."

When she was done, Zara sat down next me, taking a moment to rest. She glanced at me, then at one of the other women busy preparing the meal, a calculating expression on her face.

"How much do you really know about my son?" she asked me.

"Not much," I admitted. "He ran away from here when he was young. I know that much. He didn't get along with his father, he told me. His father—your husband—is a devout and zealous worshipper of Elohim, and that caused a rift between them."

Zara nodded. "True enough, if lacking in the details. Yes, they disagreed over many things, Elohim especially. Japheth thought his father was too . . . strict. He thought he should be able to do things his own way, and naturally Noah didn't agree. My husband is . . . very devoted to Elohim, and sometimes he loses sight of how his devotion affects the rest of us, but he means well." She paused. "The trouble is, they are too much alike. So hardheaded, those men."

"That's what Japheth said." I felt drowsy

suddenly, exhausted. "I hope my presence doesn't cause trouble for your family. Japheth . . . I care about him, very much."

Zara nodded. "I can see that, and he cares about you as well. Don't worry yourself, child. Rest. Things will work out, you shall see."

Before my eyes slid closed, I saw Zara pat the other woman on the shoulder, the same woman to whom she'd glanced earlier. This woman was young, and pretty enough in a plain sort of way, with long, straight brown hair and wide brown eyes. She seemed sad somehow, resigned. I was falling asleep, but a thought niggled at me, keeping me awake for another few minutes.

There was something that didn't make sense, but I couldn't place what it was. I forced my eyes to stay open, looking around the room. Both of Japheth's brothers were in the living area now, along with Zara and the three women. One of them was working with Shem, the older brother, their motions together practiced and comfortable, the way she glanced at him loving, familiar; Shem's wife then. The next woman was talking with the younger brother, Ham, and they too seemed close and comfortable, obviously married as well. That left Zara and the third woman. Zara was Noah's wife . . . so who was the third woman?

Zara was speaking to her with familiarity, in

close enough proximity to demonstrate comfort with each other. The girl was clearly not a maid-servant, but she didn't resemble any of the men, or Zara, so I didn't place her as a sister.

I looked again at the three women, and I saw the resemblance then. The three women were all sisters. A wife for Shem, a wife for Ham . . .

The third woman, then, was . . . Japheth's wife?

He was married?

# CHAPTER 10

## Ark

> "'Make yourself an ark of gopher wood.'"
> Genesis 6:14 (ESV)

JAPHETH WALKED THE LENGTH OF THE BOAT, running his hand along the smooth wood of the rib spars. It was clearly a boat, although the sheer size of it left Japheth dizzy. He'd seen other boats in various stages of construction, and the Euphrates River was constantly busy with ships transporting goods from city to city. There was no mistaking that this was a huge boat, but it didn't look anything like the average vessel.

Never mind the mammoth size of it, Japheth simply couldn't figure out the purpose of it. It was too long to be used in the Euphrates, that much was clear. It looked to be over four hundred feet long, which would cause it to catch on the curves of the river, even assuming there was any way to get it to the river in the first place—a two or three day journey under the best of circumstances.

"Amazing, is it not?" Noah's voice, rumbled beside him.

"Yes, it's . . . incredible. But . . . what *is* it?"

"It is a boat. An ark."

"Well, yes, I see that it's a boat, but . . . *why*?" Japheth turned to regard Noah, who stood next to him, tracing the wood grain with his palm.

"That, my son, is a long and complicated story best told another time." Noah thumped the ark with his hand and strode away. "Walk with me, Japheth."

They followed the length of the ark away from the house and crossed the plain toward the hills in the distance. Japheth sensed his father was preparing to speak, so he kept silent and waited.

"I will not apologize for my beliefs," Noah said. "My life has ever been guided by the hand of Elohim, and I shall not waver in my devotion to Him."

"I'm not asking you to apologize—"

"Be silent and listen," Noah cut in. "The ark, it is my life's work now. I began construction one year ago, alone. I had only Ham with me then, and he refused to help . . . he was even more blockheaded than you about Elohim, if you can believe that. I don't expect you to understand, especially about the ark, but I have learned a few things in the past year. Namus, he doesn't understand. The people of the village," Noah waved a hand to the north, gesturing at the small village that lay a half-hour's walk away, "they think I am mad, of course. They come to watch me work, and they mock and throw stones and rotten fruit. I have learned some measure of patience, which, as you may know, is not my strongest trait."

Japheth was listening in stunned silence. Noah had begun this speech by saying he wouldn't apologize, yet it sounded as if that was exactly what he was leading up to. Japheth nodded, but didn't interrupt.

"Japheth, my son . . . what I'm trying to say is . . ." Noah trailed off, thinking, and then began again. "While I will not apologize for *what* I believe, I will apologize for *how* I believed, when you were young. I have often thought of trying to find you, but . . . I thought you might still be angry with me. I was so stubborn, then. Hardheaded and unbending. You're the same, I know, and . . ."

Japheth waited, but Noah remained silent, watching thunderheads roll in from the hills, lightning flashing in the distance, rain sweeping the clouds into curved layers.

"I'm not sure what to say," Japheth said, finally. "I have missed you, and mother, especially. I've wished

I could come home a hundred times over the years, but the thought of facing you always stopped me. I was a fool, a hot-headed boy—"

"We were both fools. Let's call it forgiven on both accounts and move on, shall we?" Noah flashed a sudden angry glare at Japheth. "This doesn't mean I forgive you for bringing that Nephilim whore into my house."

"She's not . . . she's not what you think. Please. Don't be like that." Japheth turned and headed back to the house, too angry to be rational and not willing to compromise the fragile peace his father had extended.

Noah remained behind for a moment and then caught up. "Then what is she like? In my experience, all Nephilim are the same."

"In your *experience*?" Japheth said, his voice mocking. "You haven't left this farm since before I was born."

Noah chuckled and shook his head. "You know nothing. I was already old when you were born, Japheth. I didn't even marry your mother until I was well into my middle years. You don't—and couldn't—know anything about my life before you were born, as I do not often speak of it. I was not always a reclusive farmer, that much I can say." He sighed. "I thought I loved a woman, once, in my youth. It was not meant to be, and though it was painful at the time when things ended, your mother is . . . she is a hundred, a thousand times that young woman. My love for your mother totally eclipses the fleeting, immature feelings I harbored for that other girl. I know . . . I know in the moment it is often difficult to see that, but—"

"I'm not a child, Father," Japheth snapped. "This isn't some infatuation of a lovesick boy."

Noah blew out an exasperated breath. "I know, Japheth. I know. I don't mean to—mock or belittle, or insult you—"

Japheth's face twisted. "Yet you call her a whore."

Noah tugged on his beard. "Perhaps that was . . . unkind. But you know my feelings regarding the Nephilim."

"I do, and having lived among them I can even sympathize. But Father, Aresia had nothing to do with any of that. She is a good woman, and I love her."

Noah shook his head. "It isn't meant to be, son. It cannot work. She is not for you, nor you for her."

"What is that supposed to mean?" Japheth asked.

"What about Neses?" Noah responded with a question of his own.

Japheth pinched the bridge of his nose, groaning in frustration. "What about her? Nothing has changed. I will not marry her. I don't love her—I love Aresia."

"There is only so much room on the ark, Japheth. Elohim has made his will clear, and I cannot gainsay his plan."

"What are you talking about? What does the ark have to do with whom I love?"

"It has everything to do with it, son, although I do not expect you to understand. Not yet. You will, in time."

Japheth felt his anger rising. "Enough with the riddles, Father! Speak plainly."

Noah only shook his head. "Not yet. You are not ready to hear it, and you will not accept it even if I did speak, as you put it, plainly." Noah put his hand on Japheth's shoulder. "I will give you the only thing I have to give you: the gift of time. The waters will not come for some time yet, so I will suffer her presence for now, and this I only offer out of love for you."

"You will *suffer* her presence?" Japheth repeated Noah's words, his voice bitter. "You will suffer her presence. How compassionate of you."

Noah clapped Japheth on the back, his expression solemn. "I can only hope you will come to understand, in time." He turned and strode away, halting after a few steps and resting his palm on the side of the ark. "I am not a foolish man, Japheth. I would not have built this vessel did I not have complete faith that He would do as He said. His will shall be carried out whether you believe or not, Japheth. You are either with us, or you are not. I cannot force you to believe."

Japheth had a thousand questions, none of which had any answers. Noah strode away, then, back to where Shem and Ham were busy at work sanding boards and cutting wood into varying lengths. He sat beside the ark for a while, watching his father and brothers laboring to build a giant boat in the middle of farmland, far from any river or sea, all for no reason that Japheth could discern, except for his father's word that Elohim had spoken to him.

Japheth wrestled with his father's words, and with what they meant. What was he supposed to do about Aresia, about Neses, and about Noah's veiled insinuations?

Later that afternoon, Japheth returned to the house.

As he entered, he saw Aresia waiting for him, wrapped in fresh bandages and clothed in a clean robe. Her face was hard and angry, her eyes flashing. He halted warily at her visible anger.

"Help me outside, Japheth," she ordered, her voice snapping with the authority of one used to issuing commands and having them obeyed.

Japheth closed the space between them, lifted her as gently as he could to her feet and wrapped his arm around her waist, supporting her weight, and helped her limp gingerly away from the house.

When they were far enough way to have privacy, she slowly and carefully lowered herself onto a pile of wood and turned to face Japheth. "Why have you never told me you are married?"

Japheth flopped to the ground next to her, cursing. "It's not like you think," he told her. "We're *not* married. They betrothed me to her when we were children, and I refused to marry her. That's part of the reason I left home."

Aresia seemed somewhat pacified at that, but still she questioned him. "Why did you not marry her? She seems a kind and lovely girl."

"It wasn't because of anything she was or wasn't that I refused to marry her, it was . . . more the principle of the thing. To be honest, I *was* attracted to her when we were first introduced, but even then, barely out of childhood, I knew what was expected of us. I refused, out of stubbornness, simply because of the fact that my parents had made the choice for me without consulting my wishes."

"I see. I suppose I can understand that," Aresia said. "Father tried to make me marry several times. When I told him I wouldd rather cut my own wrists than marry a monster like Sin-Iddim—and actually tried to do so at least once—well . . . I suppose that made him see I was serious."

Japheth took her wrists in his hands and examined them, seeing a pair of faint lines crossing her left wrist. "You tried to kill yourself?"

"I would not say I tried to kill myself." She traced the lines. "It was more to prove a point to Father than to really hurt myself. I was terrified when I did this to myself. But then, I was more terrified of Sin-Iddim."

"With good reason, it seems."

"Yes, so it would seem." Aresia looked away, picking splinters from the wood beneath her.

"Can I ask—?" Japheth began.

"JAPHETH! ARESIA!" Zara's voice echoed from house, interrupting him. "COME EAT!"

Japheth helped Aresia to her feet, and they walked together back through the grass. "Later, perhaps," he said.

Aresia nodded. "I am not ready for too many questions, anyway, Japheth. Not yet."

Within the house, Neses, Ne'eletama, and Sedele were setting dishes of food around the long, low table that was the centerpiece of the dwelling. Noah, Shem, and Ham were all lounging at the table already, picking at a loaf of bread as they conversed. Japheth entered first, and a few pairs of eyes glanced up at him, acknowledging and welcoming him. And then, when Aresia entered, ducking awkwardly to fit under the low lintel, Noah, Shem, and Ham ceased speaking, and Ne'eletama and Sedele froze in the act of placing the last dishes on the table. All eyes were locked on her, staring, apprehensive and judgmental. Aresia noticed this, and Japheth felt her tense under his arm.

He hissed in irritation. "Your behavior is insulting," he barked. "She has done nothing to any of you to deserve this treatment."

Zara bustled over and guided Aresia to a nest of pillows arranged near the table. "Sit, child, sit. You are welcome at this table."

Aresia lowered herself slowly through visibly excruciating pain to the floor, working to keep her expression neutral as she settled in. Her brow was dotted with sweat and her breathing was labored as she arranged her robe. She met the eyes of everyone in turn, Zara first, with a smile, then Japheth, and then Sedele, Shem, Ham, Ne'eletama, then Noah, and Neses last.

"I am an intruder here," Aresia said, at last. "There is no need to pretend otherwise."

"You have lived among her kind for a long time," Ham said to Japheth. "For those of who have not spent so much time around Nephilim, it is somewhat disconcerting."

Zara's gaze raked around the table. "Enough of

this. Aresia is welcome at this table." She repeated her earlier statement, this time voiced as a command, her tone brooking no dissent.

Heads nodded in assent, yet eyes were cast aside, and Aresia only sighed.

"Do not trouble yourself on my behalf, Zara," Aresia murmured. "I do not expect a warm welcome."

"To be welcoming of guests and to show compassion is not a trouble, child," Zara said, staring hard at her husband. "It is merely what Elohim would expect of us."

Silence then, thick and tense and uncomfortable. Eventually, Noah cleared his throat, his gaze going around the table. "Welcome, Aresia."

A brief hesitation, and then Shem, Ham, Sedele, and Ne'eletama each murmured, "Welcome, Aresia."

Neses alone remained silent, but her gaze was steady and even, her expression open, curious even, though even to Japheth's eyes there was pain as well in her features and posture.

A moment passed and then Noah gave the blessing of thanks for Japheth's safe return and the plentiful food before them.

Zara clapped her hands together. "There. Now that we have gotten basic manners out of the way, let us eat!"

The clamor of assent then was much more

enthusiastic, conversation resuming in a wave of appreciation. Zara served Noah first, and then once he had received his meal, she personally served each person herself in turn. The meal was a long affair, and awkwardness prevailed at first, conversation stilted. Slowly, however, everyone became accustomed to Aresia's presence, and conversation flowed once more, though most of it circled around Aresia, floating past her, and she did not seem interested in attempting to join in. Japheth too remained aloof, watching his brothers with their wives, watching the ease with which everyone else interacted, their conversations easy from years of familiarity. One other, however, was often silent, seeming content to watch and listen rather than participate: Neses.

By the time the food was gone and the dishes cleared, night had fallen and darkness pervaded.

Noah tossed a log onto the fire, and the family gathered round the crackling flames.

"The world is a corrupt place," Noah said, his face lit by the leaping yellow flames, "and Elohim cannot any longer stomach the stench of sin in His nostrils. Man's time upon this earth is short. Soon, all will be wiped away by floodwaters. Nothing will remain."

Noah poked at the embers with a long, weathered stick, its tip blackened and cracked and hard from years of fire-prodding. The embers flared, sparked and spat orange flecks. Noah's face was a rough thing in the dim light, all angles like chipped stone and deep lines like crevasses.

Japheth lay with his head propped on his hand; Aresia curled in sleep in front of him. His brothers were spaced around the fire; their wives also asleep nearby. Zara sat cross-legged next to her husband, listening and staring at the coals. Neses sat away from the fire, in the shadows, her hair in a thick braid dangling over a shoulder, her eyes downcast, intent on scraping the hide of the sheep slaughtered for the evening meal.

"If He is wiping the earth clean of His creation, then why the boat?" Japheth asked.

Noah jabbed the fire in irritation. "It is an ark, Japheth. A boat is a vessel built for a journey, meant to arrive somewhere, to go somewhere. The ark is meant only to float upon the floodwaters." He stabbed the fire again, but less vehemently. "I build the ark on His command."

"Why is the ark so big, then? If it is only meant for you, why is it so big?"

"It is not meant only for me," Noah answered. "Elohim spoke to me, one night. I was out in the fields, watching stars fall from the sky in a silver rain, and I heard His voice. All my life I have believed in Elohim. My father Lamech, my grandfather Methuselah, and his father Enoch . . . all of them walked with The One God. Enoch, he was taken from this life without death, removed to the heavens by the very hand of Elohim. Long have I worshipped, long have I prayed, and long have I believed. But never had I heard the voice of Elohim with my own ears."

A pause, as Noah recalled the moment, his gaze vacant, remembering, staring into the fire. "He spoke with the voice of the stars, and their lights pulsed at His breath. The moon shone brighter with His words, until it was blinding. He spoke to me, Japheth—His words . . . touched my soul. He has . . . Elohim has made a covenant with me.

"He spoke to me, and He said: 'Behold, I will bring a flood of waters upon the earth to destroy all flesh which is the breath of life under heaven. Everything that is on the earth shall die. But I will establish my covenant with you, and you shall come into the ark, you, your sons, your wife, and your sons' wives with you. And every living thing of all flesh, you shall bring two of every sort into the ark to keep them alive with you.'"

"So . . . you're building this ark, and you're going to fill it with animals, and then all of us are going to get on it, and then, what? Some kind of flood will come? It will rain for months, or years? And we are meant to live on this boat? For how long? How does this work?" Japheth was struggling to keep his voice level, but none of it made any sense. "How are you supposed to get the animals onto the boat? And what about the dangerous ones? Will you bring the lions, too? Will they come to your call like a palace dog?"

"You mock, Japheth," Noah said, with more patience than Japheth remembered him ever possessing, "But you do not mock me, you mock The One God. The truth is . . . I don't know. I don't know how it will all work. I don't know how the animals will get onto the boat, or how the waters will come, or for how long, or anything. All I know is what Elohim has told me—build the ark, He said, so I build the ark. He is Elohim, The One God, the Creator, He of many names and all names and the One Name. If He wishes to bring two of every animal on this ark, then He will do so. He made them all with His voice and His breath, just as He made you and me and all things. Do not mock the will of The One God, son."

"I'm sorry, Father," Japheth said, truthfully. "I didn't mean to mock. I just find it . . . hard to believe."

Noah shrugged. "Your belief is not necessary. His will remains true and constant, whether you believe or not. I have my work, and I will do it whether you assist or not. Shem came a year ago, and he, much like you, mocked and remained skeptical, but now he too believes. Ham believes. Your mother, and Sedela, and Ne'eletama, they all believe."

"And what about you, Neses?" Japheth looked at Neses, glancing at her for the first time. "What do you think?"

She started at the sound of her name from his lips, and then looked up hesitantly, gazing into his eyes for a long moment. He saw hurt, and disapproval, and anger there.

"I believe Elohim can do all things," Her voice was small and quiet, but confident. "Elohim has not spoken to me in an audible voice as He did Noah, but . . . I have heard His voice nonetheless. His will does not depend on our approval."

Japheth shifted uncomfortably. Her eyes remained on him, watching him, examining him; she was supposed to be his wife, but he held another woman in his arms. Neses's eyes flicked down to Aresia and then back up to Japheth, the pain in her eyes deepening and sharpening until she returned her gaze to the hide she was scraping.

"I cannot tell you what to believe, my son," Noah said, after a long, awkward silence. "If you do not believe, then do not help build the ark. But, if you are to remain here, under my roof, then you must help the family in some way. You can help with the harvest, perhaps."

"I thought you said we had to remain apart?" Japheth asked.

"I did, and I would prefer it, but we don't have the time to build a separate dwelling." Noah glanced at Neses, who was scraping the hide with more force than was necessary. "It is unfortunate, but it is the way it must be."

Neses looked up, feeling Noah's eyes on her. "I have accepted my lot in this life, Noah. Do not seek to spare my feelings."

Japheth looked from Neses to his father, and then at his mother. Zara was looking at Japheth with the same disapproval and hurt as Neses had given him. He cursed under his breath, slipped his arm free of Aresia, and left the house.

Beyond the walls and away from the fire it was cold. Stars winked and flashed in their millions above him, each one seeming to glare at Japheth with disapproval. What was he doing wrong? He never loved Neses, and he didn't think she had ever cared for him any more than he did her—it was an arranged marriage. He'd known her for many years and liked her well enough, but he simply did not love her, and refused to marry someone simply because his father said so.

Shem came out after a moment, holding a wineskin in one hand. He took a swig and passed it to Japheth without a word, and Japheth drank, grateful for the burn on his throat and the heaviness in his stomach.

"She loves you, brother," Shem said, his voice a sudden rasp in the darkness. "Neses, I mean. She's always loved you. She was heartbroken when you left. She wept for weeks, thinking it was her you were rejecting. Mother eventually helped her realize the problem was between you and Father, but it didn't help, and she just . . . never left. She is as much a part of the family now as Ne'eletama or my own wife."

Japheth stared at Shem, disbelieving. "She barely knows me! How can she love me?"

Shem smirked in the darkness, rubbing his scar with a thumb. "That Nephilim princess of yours, how long did it take before you knew you loved her? Did you need years together to know? I think not. Give me the wineskin back . . . Father disapproves of wine, so I must drink in secret."

Japheth handed over the skin. "Well, what am I to do? I love Aresia, and she loves me. I can't go anywhere else."

"Why not?"

"Gods, Shem. Do you have any idea how complicated that is?" Japheth took back the skin and drank, feeling a lightheadedness set in. "No, I don't suppose you do. She's King Emmen's daughter, you know that. But she was also married to Sin-Iddim. She did it to protect me, because Emmen-Utu found out I was a worshipper of Elohim."

"I thought you had forsaken Elohim," Shem said.

"I did, but things . . . changed." Japheth gave a quizzical look. "How did you know about my feelings for Elohim?"

"I left home too, not long after you did, and I only came back last harvest. I lived in Bad-Tibira most of the time. I apprenticed to a metalworker, and eventually had my own business. At least, until that foolish war with Larsa."

"You fought in that?"

Shem nodded, tracing his scar. "Got this from a Nephilim arrow. Nearly killed me. You know, I saw you in Bad-Tibira a hundred times, but you never saw me. I fought in the same unit as you, three rows back. I watched you take out those Nephilim like they were mere mortal men. The men in my unit, they spoke of you with awe after that. You were an idol to them, but you never knew it . . . and then you disappeared."

"I found work with a mercenary company," Japheth answered. "It frequently took me away from Bad-Tibira."

Shem strode away, took a long piss into the grass, and then returned, staring up at the bright wash of silver stars. "Neses is a good woman, Japheth," he said, eventually. "No one can make you love her, but . . . don't hurt her any more than you already have.

She's been through enough."

"What does that mean? And how would I hurt her?"

Shem shot Japheth a frustrated scowl. "Are you dense? I told you, she still loves you. She always has. Seeing you with that princess, Aresia? It hurts her. Can't you see that?"

"I suppose. But what did you mean, she's been through enough?"

Shem shook his head. "That's her business, not mine and certainly not yours. If she wants to tell you, she will—I surely won't. Just . . . have some tact, will you?" Shem turned to go back into the house, but stopped, and spoke over his shoulder. "And just so you know, when the floods come, Father won't let your Nephilim girl onto the ark. She's part of the corruption Elohim is wiping out, Father would say. Remember what he said Elohim told him? 'Your wife, and your sons, and your son's wives.' You know what that means, in his eyes, whether you agree or no. He's softened some these past years, but not *that* much."

Shem went back inside, leaving the nearly empty wineskin with Japheth.

The stars continued their bright gaze. Japheth drained the wineskin, and tried to count the stars above his head. He passed a thousand, and then another thousand before he lost count and began again. The skies lightened to gray and the stars began to fade, but Japheth was no closer to knowing what to do, or what to believe.

When he returned to the house, the fire was stoked and the sound of snores echoed. Aresia, alone, was left awake, sitting near the fire pit where she'd been, the embers casting an orange glow on her features. She did not look up as he sat beside her.

After a few moments of silence, Japheth said, "I understand if you don't want to talk about this, but . . . what happened?"

Aresia shook her head, wiped her eyes with the back of her wrist. "As you say, I have no wish to talk about it. I want to forget."

"But you can't, can you?" Aresia didn't answer, and Japheth kept speaking. "Listen, I know how that feels. I mean, I don't know what you went through, not specifically, and I know there are things you experienced that I haven't . . . but I do understand."

"You think so?"

"There are things that keep me awake at night. Memories I can't escape, no matter how far I go, no matter how much wine I drink." He fell silent, thinking of the temple whore from Ur, the priest lapping at her blood as it spurted from her throat.

He felt Aresia's eyes on him, knew she could see his pain.

"Well, you can probably imagine, then, what happened to me, and you would be right." Aresia shuddered. "Picture the worst, most brutal things one person can do to another, and he did them to me. He forced himself on me, day and night. He sodomized little boys in front of me. He beat me and he tortured me. He did everything but kill me, and that was not for lack of trying."

"He impregnated you," Japheth stated, and Aresia only nodded. "And you got rid of it."

"Of course I did," she spat, bitterly. "Such a child would have been an abomination. I could not love such a thing. Perhaps that makes me a bad person, but I cannot make myself regret it, even if I do feel Elohim judging me for it. I would not choose otherwise, were I made to choose again."

"I would not assume Elohim judges you ill for that," Japheth said. "I do not."

"You are not Elohim. But I am glad you do not think less of me for it."

Silence.

"What happened to Irkalla? Neither she nor . . . what was his name . . . the soldier from Larsa who was driving the wagon . . . Uresh? Neither of them would speak of it."

"Oh, that poor girl. Inanna—I mean . . . Elohim

be with her." Aresia dug at the dirt with her toe. "It was awful. Worse than what happened to me, in some ways. Sin-Iddim had done his worst to me, and Ereshkigal himself could not have devised worse torture. I wanted to die. I had killed the child inside me, and he was torturing me for denying him his heir. He had executed the healer who provided the herbs, and Irkalla couldn't bear to watch me waste away, I suppose, so she devised a way to get me out.

"She had arranged to make sure one of the gates would be unguarded at a specific hour, but her plan didn't work as expected. She found Uresh, somehow, and convinced him to carry me out. I don't know how. I remember nothing from Larsa but pain, and being carried out of the palace in the dead of night. We came to the gate, which I suppose was meant to be unguarded, but it wasn't. There was a guard there, the gate captain himself. He knew me, and knew what Irkalla was doing. She . . . he made her pay with the only coin she possessed: her body. Right there at the gate, in the dirt, in front of me, and Uresh who was carrying me in his arms."

"Gods, Aresia. I'm so sorry."

"It's not your fault."

He lifted a shoulder. "In some ways . . . it is."

Aresia did not disagree with him, and there was only silence between them, then.

"This boat of your father's . . . the flood he speaks of. What do you make of it?" Aresia asked, at long last.

Japheth could only shrug. "I do not know. I have been thinking on that same question myself, and I have no answer."

Aresia stared at the orange cinders. "I heard the Voice of Elohim, Japheth. I fear your father's faith is not idle."

"Why do you fear that?"

She turned her gaze to him. "Because . . . I am Nephilim."

Japheth had no answer for that, and she clearly did not expect one from him, for she lay down, near Japheth but not cuddled against him, as had once been their wont between moments of passion. Japheth listened to her breathing slow to soft, gentle snores, the quiet sounds mingling with the other snores. He himself lay awake for a long, long time, his mind spinning, turning over the question of what he believed, what it meant, and what he was supposed to do about any of it.

# CHAPTER 11

## The Covenant

"But I will establish my covenant with you, and
you shall come into the ark, you, your sons,
your wife, and your sons' wives with you."
Genesis 6:18 (ESV)

JAPHETH WOULD NOT TOUCH ME. IN THE WEEKS
since we had been at Noah's home he had not
held my hand. He slept near me at night, but not
intimately, not comfortingly. I sensed a change in
him, but he would not even speak with me. He left
me every day to work on the Ark or to farm the
fields, and I remained behind with his mother and
sisters-in-law.

I was healing well enough, and I could breathe
without pain now. I could lay with him if he would
seek me out in such a way, yet he did not. In truth, I

did not know if I want him to be that close. I loved him and I knew, in my mind and my heart, that he loved me as well, but . . . the thought of his body against mine brought apprehension and fear, and memories of Sin-Iddim. I tried to imagine what it would be like to feel Japheth above me, looking at me with love, but all I could see was Sin-Iddim's eyes, hard and angry and brutal.

I knew Japheth was not himself, and a part of me wanted to beg him to love me and wash away the memory of that monster . . . but I could not bring myself to do so. Japheth, too, seemed reluctant. I did not know whether that was on my behalf, knowing what I have suffered, or whether it was due to the presence of that human girl, Neses.

She was a pretty girl, not lovely and not beautiful, but certainly pretty. She rarely spoke, often for days at a time; she moved with a demure grace, and she was always busy. Scraping hides, mending robes, weaving rope from flax or hemp, cooking . . . she was never still. Her hands fluttered like birds all the day long, working, working, working.

I could not stop myself from watching her. It unnerved her, I thought. I wished I could help these women with the work they did, but I have never done any of those things and even if I could I was not sure they would want my help.

Japheth worked outdoors every day, leaving at

dawn and returning for the evening meal. He came back with his tunic off, wearing only a linen kilt around his hips. His chest was oiled with sweat, his muscles gleaming and hard. I could not help but admire him.

Neses, too, watched him. She loved him, I knew she did. She hid it, and she was resigned to his indifference toward her. But still, she could not help herself from watching him in the fields as he harvested—as I did—watching him bending and swiping his sickle, gathering, stacking, and straightening, wiping sweat from his brow and hair from his eyes.

He never looked at her, never spoke to her, never even turned his body toward her. He sat on the opposite side of the fire from her at night, when we all gathered around the flickering flames to eat and drink and talk. But he was aware of her—I could see that, and so could she. And it hurt her deeply.

One day, when the men were in the field and the other women were fetching water from the well, Neses approached me, not quite daring to look at me.

She stammered a handful of words, then heaved a breath and spoke again, clearly this time. "Why do you stare at me? Have I offended you in some way?"

"No . . . you have done nothing." I shook my head, unable to formulate a better answer. "It is not anything like that."

"Then what? Do you not already have that which is supposed to be mine?" The words dropped from her lips, and she slapped a hand across her mouth, as if to take them back.

"I suppose I do, but I do not think I took him from you." I allowed my own painful truth to escape from my lips. "And really, *do* I have him? He pays as little attention to me as he does to you, lately."

She nodded, eyes downcast. "I have noticed."

"I am sorry if I remind you of . . . of what should have been. I do not mean to cause you pain."

"It isn't you, it's him. He . . . he never wanted me." The agony in her voice pained me.

"I do not think it was that," I said, "so much as his rebellion against his father."

She nodded. "I know. Zara has told me this many times, but that does not change the way I feel."

"You love him." It was not a question, and it was not a kind thing to say to her.

She only nodded again, a bare sliver of movement. "Always." She looked up at me, her eyes intense now. "If you can make him happy, then do as you will, and spare no worry for me. He deserves happiness."

"Do you not also deserve happiness?" I ask.

"My happiness is not found on this earth. I have found peace in Elohim." There is no pretense in this statement, no falsity or piety, only a deeply felt truth.

But there was peace in Neses' eyes—pain as well, old and resigned—but it was all leavened by a peace, which I envied her.

I had a feeling of impending doom, a heaviness in my heart. I did not understand it, could not divine its source, but it haunted me day and night. In the weeks since Japheth brought me to his childhood home, I had healed as much physically as I ever would, even though I knew some pain would always be with me. I still felt a dizziness I could not shake, and my vision was often cloudy. Emotionally, I knew I was still fragile. When the men moved too suddenly, I flinched. I cowered if they shouted, which Japheth and Noah often did, as men who were much alike were wont to do. They forgot their anger just as quickly as it rose, and I thought Japheth and his father were finding a peace they both needed.

Shem and Ham did not quite ignore me, but neither did they seek me out or treat me with the same familiarity as they did each other's wives. Noah was uncomfortable around me, if not openly antagonistic; he tolerated me, I thought, and no more. Zara was . . . Zara. Kind always, and thoughtful, ever making attempts to draw me in and make me comfortable.

And Japheth?

He saw me, I knew. The spark of attraction that drew us together was still there. I felt the renewed need for comfort. Perhaps not intimacy, not in the sexual sense—I remained unsure if I was capable of that, or if I ever would be. But I needed his presence. I needed time alone with him, away from his family, away from the silent judgement of Noah, and the way the brother's wives, Sedele and Ne'eletama, pretended I did not exist.

I did not know what I needed. I did not know what I wanted. I did not know where I belonged. I just knew . . . I was discontent.

I could wait no longer; I needed to feel comfort. The nightmares came every night, *Sin-Iddim's* face, angry and brutal. His hands on me—unrelenting. I needed to feel loved, and only Japheth could provide that.

I wrapped some wineskins, given me by Shem, in a blanket, and packed some food in a basket. I waited in the warm afternoon sunlight for Japheth to return from the fields.

As evening neared Japheth returned, clad in nothing but his linen kilt, his upper torso bare and muscular and sweaty, his black curls damp and tangled and falling across his eyes. He stopped at the barrel of water outside the door of the family home, splashing his face, scrubbing himself, over and over.

Straightening, droplets of water trickling down his chest, my breath caught, just looking at him.

He saw me then, sitting on the yoke of the plow a few feet away, watching him.

"Aresia . . ." he eyed the basket, "are you going somewhere?"

I shrugged one shoulder and glanced out at the rolling hills beyond the plowed field. "I would like to take a walk together. I packed some food." I lifted the basket, unnecessarily.

He blinked at me for a moment and then nodded. "Very well. Let me change, first."

I shrugged, risking a small smile. "No need."

I thought Japheth understood what I meant by that—his lightning-blue eyes flashed, and a ghost of a smile touched the corners of his lips, and I felt a moment of hope. But then his gaze darkened.

He rolled a shoulder. "A moment, only." He averted his gaze, conflict in his posture.

I sighed as he turned away, ducking under the low lintel. He returned a moment later, buckling his belt over his sleeveless tunic. He took the basket of food from me, lifted it to his shoulder, and stood gazing at me.

"Ready?" he asked.

I nodded, and we set out, skirting the plowed and planted field. Beyond it, the hills rolled like gentle waves of verdant earth, waist-high grass waving in the gentle, ever-present breeze. Into that tall grass we walked, the stalks brushing my hips. It was a beautiful day, the sky clear of clouds, an endless azure bowl above our heads. The silence between us was tense, awkward in a way it had never been before. In the months before our discovery and Japheth's capture, we often spent quiet time together, and were both content to simply be together in that silence. We hadn't needed constant conversation to be at peace together. Now, however, the silence was palpable, our comfort together broken.

There was a distance between us. A realization that, perhaps, all we'd shared was a physical connection. I didn't understand his family, and I certainly didn't understand his father. His brothers were simple enough: I was Nephilim, and thus the same as all my kind—brutal, savage, amoral, and godless in my worship of so many gods. To Zara, I was a creature to pitied. To Sedele and Ne'eletama, I was not worth considering, a thing that barely existed. And to Neses? I was less sure of her than anyone else.

And to Japheth? For a while, I'd believed we loved each other. While I was in the hands of Sin-Iddim, the thought of Japheth's love, his body, his touch, his kiss, his presence . . . it had succored me. Comforted me. But now . . . I doubted it.

We'd been walking together now for several leagues, and neither of us had said a single word.

We may as well have been walking on our own.

After another half a league of unbearably thick silence, I could stand it no more. "Japheth, stop. Put the basket down."

He nodded, setting the basket on the ground, making a clearing in the tall grass, and then began withdrawing food. He did not look at me; it was as if this was merely . . . somewhere to have a meal.

I sat down in the grass and watched him for a moment, willing him to glance my way. When he did not, I put my hand on his arm, stopping him. "Japheth . . . why—why do you not look at me?"

He turned his gaze to me, shifting backward to sit facing me, the basket between us. "I am looking at you, Aresia."

"I feel . . ." I sighed and started over. "I feel as if I do not exist to you any longer."

"You exist, Aresia. You are here."

I felt the urge to snarl at him but did not. "You cannot merely counter everything I say with the opposite, Japheth. What I feel cannot be erased or soothed with quick denials."

He sighed. "Then what? What do I say? What do you want me to say?"

"The truth?" I suggested. "You do not see me any longer. You do not touch me."

"You've been healing—"

"It has been months, Japheth. I am as healed as

216

I can ever be. Some hurts will never heal, but . . . others, they . . . they need healing of a kind mere time cannot provide." I nudged the basket aside, so there was nothing between us. "Do you know I have nightmares, Japheth? Are you aware that I wake up every night crying? Losing the child, the agony so terrible death would have been preferable . . . Mirra's head in a basket, delivered to my rooms. Irkalla, bribing the gate captain with her own body. I live all of it over and over again, Japheth, every night.

"But now I'm surrounded by your family, and they—they hate me. Your brothers hate me, and your father despises me, but I've done nothing to him . . . or to *any* of them. Only your mother treats me with any kind of decency. And Neses, oddly enough—she too accords me some semblance of . . . basic kindness. Even you—it seems you'd rather spend your days in the field, working, than with me. I have no place, Japheth! I have . . . I have nothing. Not even you, it seems."

Japheth was silent for so long I wondered if he'd gone deaf or mute. But then he heaved a sigh, and finally turned his gaze from the grass to my eyes. "I cannot erase those memories, Aresia."

"I know, but . . . can you not even attempt to—to soothe them?"

"How?"

"Hold me? Touch me? Kiss me?" My voice

cracked on the last word.

He shrugged a shoulder uncomfortably. "I—after what happened, I thought—" He sighed again. "I didn't think you'd want me to."

I inched closer to him, taking his hands. "What we had before—the way things used to be between us . . . I do not know if it can be that way again. Or if I am even capable of that kind of intimacy, yet . . ." I blinked against the pain in my heart, the onslaught of loneliness I'd been feeling for so many weeks. "I need comfort, Japheth. Something. Anything."

Again he was silent again for a long time. "I—I don't know that I have any comfort to give, Aresia. I am changed. Losing you, knowing you were given to Sin-Iddim in exchange for my life, the things that happened to me in Ur . . . all of that has altered me. And not for the better." He said this last in a whisper, his face downcast, his curls obscuring his eyes.

"Then . . . then perhaps we can—then perhaps we can comfort each other." I shifted a little closer.

He tensed. "Aresia—I . . ." He shook his head, his jaws grinding together so hard I heard them creak. "I cannot."

I sighed and felt something in my heart crack. "Then why bring me here?" I fought the shattering of my heart, fought the heaviness in my soul. "Why bring me here, just to abandon me?"

He didn't look at me, just plucked at the grass

near his knees, shoulders slumped; the mighty warrior looked . . . defeated. Broken. "I am sorry, Aresia. Truly."

I stared at him for a long time, trying to summon anything for him besides anger. "You should have left me in Bad-Tibira, then."

I stood up and walked away, back to the long, low structure of the house, past the skeleton of Noah's giant, absurd boat, towering like a mammoth skeleton of some long-dead behemoth. My feet hurt from the walk, the still tender soles throbbing but I ignored the pain, returning as quickly as I could back toward the house.

As I approached, the thought of entering that dark, low building filled me with loathing. The thought of sitting in a corner near the small, crackling fire, smoke in my eyes, the roof inches from the top of my head, Sedele and Ne'eletama pretending not to see me, Neses ghosting about in her ever-busy manner, Zara trying futilely to smooth things over . . . I couldn't do it.

The sun had not set yet so I walked away from the house, making for the boat. Shem was on a scaffold near the top, mallet pounding, the thumping echoing in staccato cracks. Ham was on the ground next to a pile of logs, using some kind of tool to separate the logs into flat boards, which Shem then fixed into place with his mallet and seed bag full of iron nails. Noah was inside the vessel with a bucket of pitch and a thick brush, painting the cracks with the tar to seal it against the water.

None of them saw me, each focused on his work, so I crept past them and found a spot in the shadow of the god-sized vessel, on the far end from where they were working. How tall was it? Forty cubits? Fifty? Hundreds of cubits long, and twice as wide as it was tall . . . a vessel so large it boggled the mind, so vast in scope that I found it difficult to comprehend how he'd even begun to construct it, much less comprehend *why*. I'd listened to their fireside discussions at night, listened to Noah speak of the instructions of his God. It was something the patriarch did nightly, repeating the words he'd heard. But still, even having heard all this every night for some months, I still didn't grasp the reason for it all.

The boat was big enough to house the entire population of Bad-Tibira . . . yet I'd heard them say that only Noah's family would be allowed on. For what reason, then? What did so few people need with a boat this size? What ocean would it sail upon? The closest river was so far away there was no possibility of getting the vessel there, and even if they could, somehow, the boat itself was so immense it would get stuck on the many curves of the Tigris and Euphrates rivers.

It was easier to wonder at Noah's folly than

Japheth's apathy. Easier to sit here, my back against a naked spar, the sun blocked out by the bulk of the partially finished vessel, wondering at Noah's madness, than to think of Japheth, refusing to look at me, to even sit close to me.

A shuffled footstep alerted me to a presence nearby; I twisted and saw Noah standing a few feet away, a bucket of pitch in one hand, the handle of the brush sticking out of the top.

He was eying me, warily, angrily. "Why are you here, Nephilim?"

"Why do you hate me, Noah?" I asked, unable to stop the words from escaping. "What have I done?"

He growled under his breath, the mustache of his gray-black beard ruffling from the huff of his breath. "You, in particular? Nothing. It is your kind. All you Nephilim, you sons and daughters of the angels, you are all corrupt and wicked. Elohim sees you all as a stain upon this earth."

"But I—"

He spoke over me, his voice gruff and harsh. "My son's spirit is broken. He will not speak of what he endured, but it was for your sake he endured it. That, perhaps, I can lay at your feet."

"What about what *I* endured, for *his* sake? Does that count for anything?" I stripped off my sandals and showed him the soles of my feet, the angry weals of a hundred burns seared into each foot.

"This, I endured for your son. Rape, I endured for him. Beatings, I endured for him. I faced death—and wished for it—for him."

Noah shifts the bucket to his other hand, eying my feet with discomfort. "For him?"

"He has spoken of none of it? Nothing?"

Noah shook his head. "Nothing. We are not so close, even now, that he would confide in me. His mother, perhaps, but not me."

I lean my head against the spar and stare up at the sky, a blue so deep it reminds me of Japheth's eyes. "We were lovers."

Noah scoffed, a brusquely sarcastic sound. "I guessed as much."

"I never expected it to last as long as it did, or that it would come to mean as much to me as it did." I close my eyes as the sun peeks over the top of the boat, bathing in me in warmth. "My father hates your kind as much as you do mine. My father saw the necklace Japheth wore, a pendant inscribed with a name of your God, and he was incensed."

Noah nodded, eyes narrowed and pinning me in place. "*YHWH.*"

He pronounced this *yo-VEH*, and when he spoke it, his eyes cast up to the heavens, and his chest filled with a great breath. The way he said it, the careful, precise enunciation of each sound . . . he rendered the simple syllables holy, somehow.

"That is not *a* name of my God, but *the* name." Noah's gaze glittered and shone as if the light of the sun itself roared behind his pupils, and his presence expanded, as if the presence of his God was somehow filling him, breathing through him. "He is **El**, The One God. He is **Elohim**, and He is **El Shaddai**, and He is **Eloah**, and He is **Elohai**. He is not *a* god, Aresia, daughter of Emmen, he is *THE* God."

Fear bolted through me. Noah's voice, as he spoke the names of God echoed, and reverberated, shuddering through the very earth as if the plates of the mountains were quaking at the sound. When Noah spoke those names, he ceased speaking as a mortal man, and spoke as the mouthpiece of the very God whose names he recited. The skies, once blue as Japheth's eyes, roiled with dark clouds black as Japheth's curls, lightning leaping in blinding bolts from cloud to cloud, and the thunder was Noah's voice. And when the juddering echoes of the names of God faded, the skies were blue once more, and I felt in the deepest pit of my belly a truth, a knowing—that Noah's Elohim was real . . . very, very real.

A profound quiet descended, then, and Noah's gaze pierced me.

"You know Him," Noah stated.

"I told you." I stared up at Noah. "I heard Him."

Noah let out a breath, setting down the bucket of pitch, and leaned a shoulder against a spar, thick arms crossed over his chest. "The necklace Zara gave Japheth . . . what about it?"

"It marked him. Had Japheth been any other human, a worshipper of Inanna and Enlil, Father perhaps would not been so angry. But the necklace marked him as a worshipper of Elohim, The One God, and my father hates them more than anyone else on this earth. But for me, my Father would have given Japheth a death longer, more painful, and more protracted than words can describe, for he was not merely a worshipper the forbidden god, but he had dared defile me, the daughter of the king. No matter that I had sought him, that I was as complicit as Japheth in our foolish affair. Have you heard the tales of what my father does to worshippers of Elohim?"

Noah nodded, his expression tight. "I have seen it."

"Compound the violence of that hatred by a thousandfold, and you might understand the fate that awaited Japheth."

"Was it worth it?" Noah asked, his voice bitter, the words dropping from his lips as if he was unable to stop them.

"Ask me that after I have finished telling you the rest," I said. "Neither of us were innocent of blame, but I knew—I *knew* I could not let Japheth suffer for my sake. So I gave my father the one thing I had which would sway him: my hand in marriage to Sin-Iddim, King of Larsa."

"His is a reign of blood and terror," Noah said.

I could only stare unseeing, barely breathing. "Any stories and rumors you may have heard . . . none of them approach the truth. You cannot fathom the horror of that place, Noah. You simply cannot."

Noah frowned, as if hearing what I wasn't able to communicate in words. "You were wed to Sin-Iddim?"

I nodded. "In exchange for Japheth's life."

Noah was silent awhile, considering me. "You love my son." It was not a question, but a statement.

I shrug one shoulder, a miserable gesture. "I do not know. I thought I did." I cast a glance up at Noah. "I do not belong here. And, as you have said, Japheth's spirit has been broken."

"But not yours?" Noah's voice was strangely soft, for so wild and gruff a man.

I blink hard against the tears—even now I found it hard to let anyone, let alone a human, see me weep.

"No. Not mine," I said.

Noah's laugh was not unkind. "Nephilim you may be—princess, queen, and descended from angels . . . but you are a poor liar, Aresia, daughter of Emmen."

I blinked up at him again. "You see through me so easily?" I wiped at my eyes. "Is this some power given you by your god, to see a person's secrets?"

"My God has granted me no power but faith, Aresia. What I see, I see because I, too, have been broken. I, too, am subject to the human condition which afflicts us all."

"What condition is that, Noah?" I asked.

He smiled, as if it should be obvious. "The fruit of the serpent, gift of Adam and Eve." He paused for effect. "Sin, Aresia."

I frowned; I'd heard the legends and tales Elohim's followers claimed as truth—creation of all things by the word of The One God, a garden, a serpent, the first man and first woman. Legends, hearsay, tales to tell in the night, nothing more. But the more I encounter this God, this Elohim, the more I wonder if all I'd heard was true.

A scrap of white cloud crossed the sun, casting a brief shadow over us, and it reminded me of the structure behind me, and my many questions.

"Why the boat, Noah?"

"You have heard what my God has told me. I have spoken of it often enough."

I shook my head. "I don't want the same story you repeat by the fire, but the truth."

He tugged at his beard, raking his fingers through the snarls. "It is the truth. He spoke to me, and he told me that the earth is filled with wicked-ness. It cannot be redeemed, cannot be saved. He bade me build this ark, because he is going to de-stroy the earth and everyone upon it."

I glance up over my shoulder at the colossal structure—the prow jutting at the heavens, the bel-ly spars bulging wide enough to swallow an entire temple. "There are nine people here, Noah. That boat you are building could carry a city."

"He is wiping out the wicked," Noah said. "He is washing clean the earth of the stain of sin, and when it is finished, He will begin anew."

I still didn't understand. And then Noah glanced out at the small pasture behind the house, in which grazed wandering clumps of oxen, a pair of onagers, a small herd of sheep, a few goats, and a scattering of clucking, pecking chickens.

"Animals," Noah said finally. "The boat is for animals."

I felt an urge to laugh, so ridiculous was the notion. "You are going to fill this ark of yours with sheep and goats and chickens?"

Noah must have heard the mirth in my voice, for he frowned at me, the expression like the gather-ing of thunderheads on the horizon. "A mated pair of every kind of animal that walks upon this earth, and two of every kind that flies over it."

"You are going to herd lions and bears and rats

and eagles onto this ark?"

Noah let out a hissing sigh, as if he had answered this question a thousand times. "He will provide a way. He always provides a way." It was the only answer he gave, lapsing into irritated silence.

"I do not mean to mock, Noah. I do not know your god. I have heard His Voice, but I do not know Him. I do not know if I believe in Him. I know He is real, but to believe in Him, after all I have experienced? It is too much." I look to the sky, as if to see this One God, Elohim, in the endless blue. "I do not mock. But neither do I understand."

Noah gazed at me steadily, for so long I became uncomfortable under his stare. Eventually, he spoke.

"He does not ask us to understand, Aresia. He asks us to have *faith*."

"In what?"

"In that which we cannot see, but feel. In that which we hear, but cannot taste. In that which is, and was, and forever will be. In *Him*, Aresia."

"I had faith in my gods," I said.

"Did they speak to you?" Noah demanded. "Did they accept your offerings and answer your many prayers?"

I shook my head. "Never. And thus I do not believe in them any longer."

"You have prayed to The One God," Noah said, his gaze refusing to release me from its potency.

"You spoke to Him, you begged something of Him, am I correct?"

Slowly, I nodded.

Noah tilted his head to one side. "And what did you ask of Him?"

"'Save him,'" I whispered. "That is what I prayed. Save him."

Noah's gaze shifted beyond me, to the fields whence I came; Japheth was returning, at long last, carrying the basket. "And there he is."

"Broken."

Noah nodded. "But what is broken can be fixed. What is shattered can be remade."

"But not as it was," I argued.

"You are not as you were at birth, or as a child, or as a young woman. You have changed, all the while. Pain changes us, and so too does pleasure, and all that exists in between. All things change us, for God formed man out of clay, and as clay we are, from birth to death, ever malleable." As he spoke he stared at Japheth, who was approaching us from a distance. "We are none of us as we were—that is life, Aresia."

"Your God . . . will He speak to me again, do you think?"

Noah shrugged. "I cannot answer for Him, for He alone knows His will."

A long silence, but for the hammering of Shem's

mallet and the scrape of Ham's adze.

And then Noah met my eyes once more, and they were full of a sadness I could not comprehend. "'You, your sons, your wife, and your son's wives,'" Noah intoned. "That is what my God told me. When the waters come, we will enter the ark, and we will ride out on the floods which will clean the earth."

I swallow hard at Noah's implication. "I see."

"I cannot change the will of God, Aresia." He stood up. "I am sorry."

# CHAPTER 12

## All Life

"'There must be a male and a female in each pair to ensure that all life will survive on the earth after the flood.'" Genesis 7:3 (NLT)

JAPHETH BOUND THE FINAL SHEAF OF WHEAT, tossed it on the stack, and wiped his brow with his wrist. It was a hot day at the end of the harvest season; he'd plowed the field, planted, weeded, and harvested the entire crop of wheat by himself, and so felt a little burst of pride at the head-high stack of golden wheat. It needed only to be threshed now, and then would be ready for Namus to collect and transport to Bad-Tibira.

After a short rest, Japheth transferred a portion of the sheaves into the back of the wagon, tossed the sickle up onto the driver's bench, and climbed up.

With a click of his tongue and a snap of the reins, the onagers lurched into motion. He was in the farthest field east, just over the rise from the house, and it only took a few minutes to crest the shallow hill, which brought the ark into view.

It was more than half-finished now, with the sides nailed into place from keel to midway up, with many of the interior compartments also in place. The more complete it became, the more staggering the scope of the undertaking became, and the more baffling the whole business was to Japheth. It wasn't that he doubted the existence of God, or that he doubted the faith of his father, it was just . . . difficult to believe a flood so monstrous would need a boat of this size.

He was a practical man, a warrior, and a farmer. If he planted a seed, cared for it, nurtured it, then it would grow into a plant; if he swung a sword, his enemy died. If the rains came, the crops would grow; if there was a drought, they died. These were constants; these were things he could count on as being true.

Faith was more difficult. He'd watched his father and mother; he'd seen their faith. He'd watched his father offer sacrifices to Elohim, watched him walking in the fields, talking to God as if speaking to a friend pacing at his side. He'd seen his father with that vacant, faraway expression that said he was listening to the Voice of God. But Japheth had never heard that voice, had never felt that presence. He'd seen the effects of His presence on Noah.

Having witnessed their unwavering faith for his entire lifetime, Japheth believed in the basic existence of Elohim. He even allowed himself to believe that some prayers had been answered—he was still alive after all, and so was Aresia.

But building a giant boat in farmland hundreds of miles from the nearest sea, because the whole earth was going to be flooded? That was harder to understand—that was harder to believe in. Yet Noah believed. Zara believed. Sedele and Ne'eletama believed. Shem believed. Ham believed. And Neses? She believed more fiercely—if more quietly—than anyone else but Noah.

After their last meeting in the fields of golden wheat, Aresia remained aloof and distant. She'd taken to sleeping under the sheltering bulk of the ark's round belly, often keeping to herself for entire days on end. Zara brought her food, and even Noah would spend time talking to her, which Japheth found supremely unsettling. Neses, too, could often be seen near Aresia's little nest of blankets, speaking in low tones. What did those two women talk about? Him? God? Japheth did not know, but he often wondered.

He spent hours awake in the dark cold, keeping

watch during the night, sitting in the open doorway of the house, staring out at the tiny orange flicker of Aresia's candle. What did she do out there, all alone? What did she think, what did she feel?

He thought of the love they shared. The fierce need to protect her, to shelter her, to see her healed, in the days following her escape from Sin-Iddim. He'd thought that was love.

But his experiences at the hand of Mesh-te still haunted him.

His work in the fields was all that could distract him, all that was able to erase the memory, even for a moment. And the only way he could fall asleep was at the bottom of a wineskin. His brothers watched him drink, and they disapproved. His parents watched him drink and disapproved even more, but they would only look at one another and turn their heads.

Staring after Aresia, night after night, he wondered what he could say to her to ease her pain. Japheth knew, deep down, that he owed her even the smallest comfort, but he was now so troubled, he had no idea how to comfort her.

The thought of touching her, after what he'd experienced, made him shudder, even thought she was now more beautiful than ever. Life away from the city, away from the horrors, was doing her wonders.

It wasn't Aresia . . . it was him. She had tried to reach out to him many times, but he spurned her and for that he was sorry. What comfort could he offer her now?

He arrived at the house with the wagonload of wheat. After seeing to the onagers and sending them out to graze, he washed his hands and face. He heard the voices of the women inside, Zara giving the occasional order, Sedele and Ne'eletama answering, telling jokes to each other, and laughing. He glanced over at the ark and saw Aresia on a scaffolding next to Noah, painting pitch on newly finished sections of siding. It appeared neither she nor Noah was speaking, but they seemed comfortable in each other's presence.

It was . . . unsettling. What had they found in common?

"She heard the voice of El," Neses said, startling him.

Japheth pivoted to find Neses standing behind him, a basket of wet clothes propped on one slim hip. She was a small, unassuming woman who barely reached his shoulder, her body thin as a reed, her hands and wrists and ankles delicate. She was like the birds that ran upon the shores of the Tigris, prone to long bouts of stillness so one forgot they were near. At other times she would be so restlessly busy it was tiring to watch her. Fresh from the nearby Euphrates tributary, she had the hem of her dress tucked into her belt, leaving her legs bare. Her hair was brown, dark and thick; she normally left it unbound, but now she had it twisted up on the top of her head, baring her neck.

Japheth blinked, taking in her presence, and then turned away as she set her basket down and released the hem of her dress.

"Who heard the Voice of El?" he asked.

"Aresia."

Japheth merely nodded his head.

Neses lifted a tunic out of the basket and wrung it out. "You watch her. At night, I mean. I see you staring after her."

"You watch me?" Japheth questioned, shooting her a sharp glance.

"I have trouble sleeping, many nights," she said, her voice quiet. "I am not watching you, I merely . . . see you."

"And how do you know it's her I watch?"

Neses let out a soft sigh; so quiet that Japheth nearly missed it. "Who else would you stare at half the night?"

She hung the garment over the side of the wagon, reached for another, and wrung it out.

"I see you talking to her, sometimes," Japheth replied.

"She is lonely." Neses looked directly at Japheth, making it seem almost an accusation.

"What do you talk about?" Japheth asked, after a moment.

"We talk about El. She has many questions. And we talk of other things."

"Like?"

"Like why you have abandoned her. Why a god would allow such horrible things to happen, both to her and to you." Neses did not look up from the clothing she was setting out to dry, but her words stung all the same. "She wonders about the many names of El, and she wonders at the purpose of life, if El is going to wash the earth clean."

"And what do you tell her?"

Neses didn't answer right away. She finished hanging a robe over the wagon and then stopped, her hands resting on the lip of the basket, her gaze finally lifting to Japheth's. "I tell her what truths I possess, which are not many.

"I do not know why you would bring her here and then abandon her so completely, among a people foreign to her. I do not know why El allows pain and horror and violence. I do not know why men kill men." She paused, swallowing hard, her gaze dropping, along with the volume of her voice. "I do not know why men rape women. Why my Lord Elohim would create such beauty in this world, and yet allow such ugliness. I do not know. I think, sometimes, that I will never know."

"I haven't abandoned her, Neses—" Japheth started.

She cut him off, quietly yet effectively. "Yes, you have." She met his eyes once more. "I see it, she sees it—we all see it. It was cruel of you to bring her here, among us, only to leave her alone so you can wallow in your own pain."

Anger boiled up inside Japheth. "You do not know what I have endured, Neses! You cannot fathom what horrors keep me awake at night."

Her wide brown eyes narrowed, her jaw tightening, her slender body stiffening. "Oh no? You think not?" She leaned forward, her fingers gripping the basket tightly. "You think you alone have lived through nightmares?"

"Of course I don't think that, but—"

She only stared at him, her expression so rife with disgust and contempt that he fell silent. "You have not earned the telling of my truths, Japheth, son of Noah. But hear this: time is short. Your days with Aresia are numbered, and that number dwindling swiftly. She knows this, and she has accepted this as well as anyone could. But what about you? Will you allow her to spend her remaining days on this earth alone, and in misery? Nephilim she may be, and El alone knows I have no cause to feel compassion for her kind, but all creatures on this earth are deserving of comfort."

Japheth felt her words hitting his heart like a hail of arrows. "What do you mean, Neses?"

She only shook her head. "You know very well what I mean, Japheth. Refuse to believe if you will, but when the floods come you will regret wasting this time."

"You truly believe the whole earth will be flooded?" he asked.

"I do." Two simple words, but Neses's quiet voice imbued them with an utter surety that pierced Japheth's doubts.

He sighed and had no response. After a moment, it became clear there was nothing else left to say. Neses, the girl he had known all his life, had given him much to think about.

Japheth turned away, and his feet carried him toward the towering hulk of the ark, its long profile a dark shadow with the sun behind it. Wedges of sunlight speared through gaps in the sides where the work was yet unfinished, laying striped paths of red and gold over the waving green of the grass. Shem's mallet echoed, as ever—*thock-thock-thock-thock . . . thock . . . thock-thock*.

Aresia was sitting in a pool of light, a pile of

rushes beside her, which she was plaiting into a basket. Her work was clumsy, the chore unfamiliar to her royal hands, but she was working steadily, her focus so total that Japheth's presence went unnoticed until he cleared his throat and shuffled a sandal in the grass.

She glanced up, and her gaze remained cold. "Japheth. Is there something you need?"

He hesitated, unsure why he was standing in front of her, or what he was going to say. "I—"

She gazed up at him, waiting. "Speak or leave."

"Do you feel I have abandoned you, Aresia?" he asked finally.

She stared at him, and then returned her gaze to her work, bending a rush into a loop to fit another through it. "To say you abandoned me would suggest a deeper relationship than I think we ever had." She frowned, realizing her plait was crooked. As she spoke she undid it, straightened the crooked piece, and tried again. "I deceived myself into thinking a bond existed between us. I now realize that was childish dreaming on my part."

Japheth absorbed her statement.

He sat facing her, set a stack of rushes in his lap, and began plaiting. "You think there was nothing between us? That there *is* nothing, even now?"

She kept her gaze on her work. "We shared physical pleasure, Japheth, nothing more. We spoke of nothing real, nothing deep. We never shared any-thing of our true selves. Our only bond was that our meetings were dangerous, and we paid the price. I was the princess, and you wore a name of the for-bidden god. I meant nothing to you, nor you to me."

"That is neither true nor fair, Aresia." He looked at her, but she refused to lift her eyes to his. "It was more than that. It was—it was becoming more than that."

"Be honest, Japheth. What we had was infatua-tion. It was lust. It was nothing."

"Then why did you marry Sin-Iddim?"

Her hands froze. Her entire being went still and stiff, but she still didn't look at him. "Because Father would only have killed you as a way of punishing me. It was unjust."

"If I meant nothing to you—if what we had meant nothing, you wouldn't have cared what happened to me." He ducked his head, trying to catch her eye. "And if you meant nothing to me, I wouldn't have risked my life for you, and I wouldn't have brought you all the way here."

"That may be true, but if you truly cared, you would have done something when I begged you for comfort!" Aresia's voice snapped like the lash of a whip, hard as stone, cold as ice, sharp as a blade.

"I should have—" Japheth started, but couldn't finish. He tried again. "I have faced many hardships, as you know. I have seen the face of Nergal coming to take me to the underworld, and yet I lived."

"What is your point, Japheth?"

"That day in Ur . . . those hours in the hands of Mesh-te, the priest—they were the darkest of my entire life. They . . . he broke me, Aresia." Japheth's voice cracked, and he swallowed hard before continuing. What Mesh-te did, *how* he did it . . . and the fact that it was merely because of the name of God on the necklace . . ."

"You never told me what happened to you."

He shook his head. "I . . ." He shook his head again. "A priest of Ereshkigal took me prisoner in Uruk. He saw that necklace, and decided to punish me just for wearing it. He brought me to his temple and hauled in a prostitute from the temple of Inanna, and he gave me herbs that . . . forced me into an arousal I did not want and could not control. I was bound to a chair, unable to move. He forced that prostitute, who was no more than a girl . . . he forced her to mount me. To show me how one is meant to worship Inanna, he said. And as she . . . performed her duties in front of the priest—he . . ." Japheth stopped, unable to continue.

Aresia was pale and horrified. "Japheth, I had no idea—"

Japheth's face twisted in a grimace. "There is more, but I will not speak of it." He choked on his breath, on the knot in his throat. "Those are terrible memories that will always be part of me."

"Just as a part of me will never leave Sin-Iddim's bed chamber."

Japheth nodded and set aside the basket he'd partially woven. "I didn't mean to abandon you, Aresia. I am broken far more than I thought—I don't know how to—"

"We can comfort each other, Japheth," Aresia said, her voice soft, quiet, tremulous, hopeful. "Just be near me. It doesn't have to be . . . *that*, just—all I need is to know that—to know I'm not—not alone."

He shifted so he was sitting beside her, the ark behind them blocking out the reddish rays of the setting sun. Wrapped his arm around her, and pulled her close. "You're not alone, Aresia."

She was stiff for a moment, and then she relaxed, shifting downward to rest her head on Japheth's shoulder. "Thank you."

The evening shadows grew long, and they remained thus, clinging to each other as the stars emerged from the darkness in a spray of luminous silver, until Aresia's head nodded, and she drifted downward onto Japheth's lap, and he continued to hold her as she slept.

In the darkness, in the deep drowning blackness of the night, away from the house and the ark both, in the waist-high grass sat a woman. Her knees were drawn up to her chest, her delicate arms wrapped around her shins. Her hair was loose, tangled in long strands around her face. She inhaled deeply, attempting to gain control of her breathing, to tamp down the pain, but the inhalation became a shudder, and a fresh wave of tears seeped from her eyes and onto her chin.

In the distance, she could see the profile of the ark outlined by the starlight. Between the wavering stalks of grass, a flame flickered. It was but a small candle, its light casting a dull orange glow easily seen against the vast infinity of the dark sky. Yet the feeble illumination was sufficient to cast shadows upon the side of the ark, like cave paintings come to life. The shadows twisted upon the walls of the ark, telling a story.

The woman, utterly alone in the wide emptiness of the fourth watch of the night, could not look away from the story unfolding on the walls of the heaven-sized vessel. She could not look away but, equally, she could not stand the pain watching.

On the wall of the ark, a hand reached up, fingers trembling. Another hand, larger and masculine, joined the first, and the fingers tangled together. A spine arched, and a knee bent. A moan quavered, long and high and then muffled, as if lips were pressed against a shoulder. A shoulder lifted, and then the shadows rolled, coiled, and shifted, and now a pair of profiles were cast upon the wall, male shoulders and a spine and hips, flexing, and beneath him long, feminine legs lifted, wrapped around those hard hips. A hand reached up, and another moan echoed, joined soon after by a low rumble. All this, told in the flickering and jumping of shadows.

Neses watched, unable to stop herself.

*Elohim*, she prayed, the plea clanging in her mind like a scream, *take this from me. Take this love away. Strip it from my heart, so I no longer feel this pain. Have I not suffered enough, my Lord? Have I not yet endured enough, El Shaddai?*

She heard no voice, felt no answer. The heavens were silent, and the cracks in her heart widened, deepened, and her tears ran like a river.

After a time, she could take no more, and stood, fleeing back to the house. She rolled into her pallet of blankets near the cook fire, but as dawn leavened the darkness with gray and pink, sleep continued to elude her.

As it always had, especially since Japheth had returned, the grip he'd always had on her foolish heart had never left.

# CHAPTER 13

## The Seventh Day

> "'Seven days from now I will make the rains
> pour down on the earth . . .'" Genesis 7: 4
> (NLT)

THE ARK WAS NEARLY COMPLETE. THE OUTER and inner surfaces had been painted with several coats of thick black pitch, until every crack and nail hole was filled and sealed against the waters. Inside, the three levels had been finished and divided into stalls and spaces, with a massive door in the side.

I marvelled anew every single day. I watched them all working together to complete construction; Zara, Sedele, Ne'eletama, and Neses all helped as well, most domestic work abandoned now. There was a sense of feverish urgency, propelled in part by the wall of black clouds gathering in the east. The men attended to the construction, while the women worked on the finer details; the men building the door and framing out the stalls and hauling in baskets and barrels of supplies while the women prepared the living space inside the ark. The more urgent the work became, the more alone I became . . . during the day, at least. At night, Japheth spent his time with me under the belly of the ark. He held me, and made love to me, and comforted me, and I soothed him to sleep and we found at least a measure of peace in each other.

I felt Neses out there, however. I knew she was watching us—but I was unsure whether Japheth was aware of her scrutiny.

During the day, Neses avoided me now, our temporary alliance formed out of my loneliness broken when Japheth came to me that night.

Storms gathered in the east, lightning flashing miles distant, echoed much later by grumbling peals of thunder. Those storms approached, and swiftly. Wind blew, now, all the time, night and day, a hard hot breath-stealing presence. The wind was alive, I sometimes thought, as I watched Noah and his family scurry about like mice. The wind blew grit in stinging curtains, crunching between my molars and gathering in the valley between my breasts and sticking in the hollows of my ears and crusting in my nostrils. The wind bent the grass flat against the soil, and in the forests to the north I heard trees crack and shatter and topple which was, I now believed, the breath of Noah's God, The One God, El.

I heard rumbling, too. Not thunder, but something else. A shuddering under my feet, as if the very earth itself was shifting, as if there was some mighty pressure gathering in the depths of the rock. Over my head, the sky was blue, always blue, cloudless and clear, but the eye was ever drawn to the east, where the thunderheads gathered in mountainous black ranges, obscuring the sky. There in the east, if I peered and squinted, I could see drifting, draping, twisting, wind-blown curtains of rain, like a wall marching ever westward toward this place.

I wondered what the locals in the nearby village thought of the wall of storms, what the cities that blackness had already engulfed were experiencing . . .

I did not doubt Noah. I did not doubt Elohim any longer. I did not doubt the coming of the flood.

But now—as I sat in the back of the wagon, watching Noah work, watching Japheth hauling basket after basket of grain, bale after bale of hay, and endless haunches of slaughtered mutton, watching Shem and Ham settle the massive door into place at the top of the ramp leading up to the middle deck, watching the women gather bundles of clothing and baskets of candles—I heard in repeating echoes Noah's words: *you, your sons, your wife, and your sons' wives . . .*

There was no doubt as to the implication—there is no place on that ark for a Nephilim. I am not Japheth's wife—neither is Neses, but they were betrothed, and have been since childhood, and Neses is a human.

Zara's eyes went to me, now and again, filled with sadness.

Japheth—I did not know what he thought, for he worked as feverishly as the rest of his family, only stopping to collapse in my arms long after sunset. He avoided my eyes, even when he moved above me.

He knew what the future held.

Later, when the day's work was done and Noah and the others slept in the house, Japheth emerged from the darkness, a candle in his hand, its light adding to that shed by the candle at my feet. He moved slowly, stiffly, as he lay down beside me. He reached for me, but for the first time, I denied him, turning my face away from his lips.

"What is it, Aresia?" he demanded.

"What will happen to me, when the flood comes?" I asked.

He rolled away from me, staring up at the stars, his arm over his eyes. "I don't know."

"Do you not?" My tone was sharper than I had intended, but I do nothing to soften it.

He sighed. "No."

"There are not so many possibilities, Japheth." I sat up, placing my back to the wood of the ark's outer wall. "When the flood comes, you and your family will enter the ark, and either I will be with you, or I will not."

He sat up too, and I gazed at him. His jaw flexed, tensed, shifting as he ground his molars together, and his thick bicep twitched as he passed a hand through his curls. "I don't *know*, Aresia."

"You *do*," I snapped, my voice a whisper. "You *do* know. Perhaps you refuse to admit it to yourself, but you know."

"My father has not spoken of it, yet."

"Look to the east, Japheth!" I shouted, suddenly angry. "The storm gathers! Have you not felt the earth shaking under your feet? You feel it, do you not? The coming of the rains? The approach of a storm such as this earth has never seen . . . *I* feel it, Japheth. You feel it too, or you would not work at so driving a pace."

"Yes, I see it. I feel it."

"And do you believe the flood will come?" I demanded.

He sighed. "Yes, I do."

"Then surely you must wonder at my place in all

of this. 'You, your sons, your wife, and your sons' wives.' Those are the words your father spoke to me, the words Elohim spoke to him."

I rose to my knees, reaching for Japheth, anger turning to fear, to terror, to desperation. "Am I your wife? Do I have a place on this ark? Or am I fated to drown when the waters come?"

He growled, backing away from me, his fingers raking through his hair yet again. "*I—do—not—know*, gods damn it!" he shouted. "What do you want me to say, Aresia? You want to hear that my father will deny you a place? That Shem has told me as much? That Sedele and Ne'eletama whisper of it at night? Is that the truth you wish to know? What am I supposed to say? We are just now learning how to love each other, and I—I cannot stop this. I feel the truth of it—of course I do! The storms in the east, they are no normal storms. The rumbling in the earth, the rains that approach? They are from El Shaddai, and I cannot stop them. What am I to do? I don't know—I don't know!"

"Make an offering to El, then, on my behalf. Pray to Him. Ask your father." I reached for Japheth, and this time he allowed me to grab hold of his arms. "I do not want to die, Japheth. I want to live. I want . . . I want to love you."

He exhaled wearily, lying back onto the grass. "I will speak to my father in the morning."

I lay down beside him, my heart beating wildly.

There was a grinding snarl, and the earth shivered beneath us, the ground itself expanding and pushing skyward so forcefully that the ark swayed on its creaking support frame, and in the distance an onager hee-hawed anxiously, its braying echoed by the blattering of a frightened goat and the worried squawking of chickens. The wind howled fiercely, battering and blowing in the darkness.

I did not sleep, all that night. Nor any night thereafter.

I found myself wandering farther and farther from the house and the ark, as work on the vessel slowed to completion. Supplies were laid in: stores of food in improbable quantity, barrels of water and barrels of wine, candles and rush torches by the hundreds—the result of work Zara, Sedele, Neses, and Ne'eletama had been doing for well over a year, if not more.

There were cages in the lower level meant for smaller animals like cats and rodents and birds and bugs and monkeys, giant stalls in the mid level, with half of the uppermost deck nearest the ceiling partitioned into bedrooms and storerooms, and the other half filled with more stalls, these not so large as the ones on the middle level, which was the largest open space in the vessel. Running the entire perimeter of the ark, just beneath the ceiling was an opening one cubit high, allowing in light and air; on one side of the vessel was a doorway in the very center of the boat, leading to the middle level. The doorway was tall enough and wide enough to allow the largest animals through, although the door itself was so large and unwieldy that I was unsure how even all four men working together would be able to close and seal it.

I had yet to see a single animal, aside from those that were part of Noah's flocks. The wind continued to howl as with the voice of an animal, and the earth rumbled and shook, yet over our heads the skies remained blue and clear. In the east, however, the black clouds roiled and menaced, thunder quaking and grumbling, rain blowing in sheets visible from miles away.

On the morning the ark was finished, I departed before dawn, bringing with me a wineskin and a rind of cheese. Noah and all his family were bustling about with renewed fervor, ferrying back and forth from the house to the ark, now emptying the long, low-roofed structure of personal belongings. Even Japheth was distracted and did not notice me as I walked away.

Across the now-fallow western field I went,

stepping over the furrows of brown, sun-dried soil. The field gave way to the waist-high grass, the high northern hills before me. An hour or more I walked, until I reached the hills, and then up into them I hiked, until I reached an outcropping of rock some hundreds of feet above the earth. I sat upon a rock, ate the cheese, drank from the wineskin, and stared out at the land.

From this vantage point, I could see for many, many miles, all of Noah's fields now fallow—the northern field, the western, the eastern, and the southern, with the long low house in the center of them all and the ark beside it, dwarfing the little house. Beyond laid green rolling hills and then more squares of farmland. I could see a thin brown line snaking its way between them—the highway leading to Bad-Tibira.

I had not thought of Father in months, nor Sin-Iddim, or any of my brothers. If this flood happened, they would all die. They would be swept away. They would have no clue what was coming. Their lives would continue as they ever had; my brothers, perhaps, would be in the city beyond the palace, whoring and dicing, as was their practice. Father would be in his throne room, hearing complaints, deciding cases, or conspiring with his generals. The people in the palace would be scurrying to and fro importantly, and in the city life would be bustling onward, people loving, hating, lying together, arguing, selling, buying, trading, children crying, old ones dying. They would be praying to Inanna and Enlil and Ereshkigal and the hundreds and thousands of other gods, their prayers rising up to the deaf heavens.

Did El hear their prayers, if they did not speak or think His name? I think not, if the flood was meant to wipe them all away. If I prayed to Him now, would he hear my prayer? I was a Nephilim. I was that which He was wiping from the earth. Why would He hear me?

*Elohim . . . El Shaddai . . . do you hear me? Does my prayer reach your ears? What is my lot in this life? Am I meant to die?*

The skies remained silent. The wind blew, and the earth rumbled, but Noah's God did not speak to me.

I sat on that rock until the sun sank low, and I did not hear the Voice of God.

I was woken by a droplet of cold on my forehead. I stretched and sat up, a rush of dizziness washing over me as I realized I was still perched on the outcropping of rock, a fall of hundreds of cubits below me should I slip . . . I'd fallen asleep. It was just before dawn, yet after the darkest hours of night, the sky just light enough to let me see the mountain be-hind me, and the fields below and before me, and the shape of the ark in the distance.

Another droplet spattered on my forehead; I looked up and saw darkness, an absence of stars, a total blackness that writhed and moiled. Bright white light flashed beside me, blinding me and sear-ing images of white and black on the backs of my eyelids. Then, a moment later, the heavens cracked apart with a shattering sound, as if the mountain was fracturing beneath me. Another droplet, and another.

I blinked in the darkness. Far to the west, an-other flash of lightning burst across the sky, a zag-ging jag of white-purple that illuminated the whole earth for a fragment of a second. In that moment, I saw the ark, as clearly as if it were a bright, clear noontime.

Moving up to the ark, toward the doorway on the far side from where I sat, was a thick dark line. It was hard to make out details from this distance, especially in the pre-dawn dark of a stormy morn-ing, but it was obvious what I was seeing. Animals, making their way onto the ark.

Another flash of lightning illuminated the earth, and I saw a giant animal, tall and wide and gray, with a long nose and flapping, twitching ears, beside it another, identical to it. I heard the roar of a tiger, and the chittering of a monkey. Above the ark, birds flew in a wheeling cloud of spiraling confusion, pairs and pairs and pairs, no two pairs the same, birds of all sizes, from the largest soaring hawks to the smallest frantic sparrows.

A spatter of raindrops pattered on my head, and then more fell, wetting my shoulder. Thunder billowed to the north, a long rolling boil of angry sound. Lightning again, southwest. Then again, northeast. I climbed higher, then, until I could see in all directions. As I pivoted in place, spinning from north to west to south to east, I saw flickers and flashes and spears and jags of lightning in every direction, bolts striking so close they cast shadows on the earth, and others so distant they seemed like the flicker of a candle. Thunder, always thunder, a continuous roll of noise, a wall of sound from every direction, thunder so constant now that it shook my bones, shook the very earth under my feet. The mountain quaked, rocks toppling and jumping and avalanching. And, in intermittent bursts, a cold rain, hints of the deluge to come.

As a girl, I remembered when a storm struck suddenly. I was playing in one of the gardens, my mother nearby. The sun was shining, the sky blue, not a cloud to be seen. And then, with a suddenness that confused my young mind, clouds flew like a flock of ravens to blot out the sun, and the winds kicked up. I felt a drop of rain and then two and then a dozen, and then thousands, too many to count, a wall of rain cascading from the heavens. My mother hurried me into the palace and we stood in the doorway watching the rain, listening to the thunder. The moment right before the rains opened up, that moment was one I remembered vividly. The rain had begun slowly, and then picked up force so swiftly.

I had that same feeling now, standing on the mountaintop, lightning flashing in every direction, thunder all around . . . except magnified a million-fold from that time as a little girl. My heart hammered in my chest, and my blood panicked in my veins.

I did not want to be here, on this mountain, when the rains came.

I did not want to die.

*Spare me, Elohim. Spare me, God of Noah.*

I heard no voice, only that of thunder.

My feet scrambling on the rock face, I descended the mountain, and when I reached flat ground, I ran, the skirt of my dress caught up around my thighs.

I ran, thunder crashing all around, droplets of rain striking like hail, fat and thick and hard.

I ran through the waist-high grasses, across the fallow fields, into the clearing around the ark, and the forgotten house. I stood some distance away, in the open, awed.

The earth was alive with movement. Creatures of all sizes were gathered in a stomping, snorting, bucking, snarling, hawing, keening mass. The doorway stood open, the ramp down, facing the far southern fields and the open meadow beyond, and in that space, a teeming throng of wildlife.

Every animal was there, jumbled and bumping together, tiny things skittering between legs and darting around hooves, tails whipping, teeth snapping. The air buzzed with life, hummed with the vibrancy of animal energy. I saw cows, aurochs, horses, onagers, long-necked, long-legged spotted things I had no name for, things that crawled on the ground with shaggy squat legs and an impossibly long nose, animals like lions but smaller, and things like the little leaping palace court monkeys except much larger. The noise was cacophonous, a bewildering assault of whinnies and brays and snarls and roars and moans and lows and chitters and chatters, chickens clucking and eagles keening and ravens haw-haw-hawing and goats blatting and so many noises and sounds I could not separate one from the other.

They teemed and boiled in the open space before the ark, but no animal disturbed another, though there was much snapping and jostling for space. Lions paced beside gazelles, teeth bared and snarling in staccato bursts. The throng crowded and moved and shifted, and those animals nearest the ramp hopped and leaped and stalked onto it, two by two, a male and a female, and as soon as there was room, the next pair of animals ascended the ramp.

There was no shepherd, no one guiding them. Noah was standing near the ramp but well away; watching with as much awe as I. Beside him, Zara clung to his waist, hand over her mouth, eyes wide. Shem and his wife Sedele, and Ham and his wife Ne'eletama were nearby as well, all watching the parade of life as it marched onto the ark.

I had an errant thought: neither Shem and Sedele nor Ham and Ne'eletama had children, yet it was clear both couples had been married for several years; a curiosity, one for which I had no answer.

Japheth was missing, and I cast my glance around the clearing, searching for him.

I saw him, after a moment, crouched in the narrow space beneath the belly of the boat, between the framework and the vessel it supported. He caught my eye, and gestured to me. I went to him, crouching near him; from this angle, the ramp blocked Noah's view of us.

"Hide here," Japheth told me. "When the animals have all boarded, my father and the others will join them. After the last animal has gone aboard the ark, make your way on after them. Hide in the lowest level. There is a space I have found, where the cages and stalls have left a gap near the prow of the boat. There is a space large enough for you. I have left food and water and a robe. You will be safe there."

I stared at him. "Sneak aboard?" I shook my head. "I will not hide in the belly of this boat like a rat in the corner of a storeroom, Japheth."

"It is the only way," he insisted. "My father would not even discuss it with me. I have prayed without ceasing and have had no answer. I offered a bullock to El, and prayed for you to be spared, and received only silence."

"Perhaps the silence is your god's answer," I whispered, my voice shaky.

He grabbed my arms and shook me. "I will *not* let you die, Aresia. Not like this." He cast his eyes heavenward. "If that is His answer, then perhaps He is not my God."

I cupped his cheek. "He *is* your God, Japheth. Do not cast aside your belief for me." I shook my head. "I will not hide."

"Please, Aresia." He moved out of the space and knelt before me. "Please. You have to. It is the only way."

I stepped away. "No, Japheth. I will *not* hide."

He visibly held back tears. "I will wait. I will wait

until the door is sealed, and when it is, I will go to the lowest level and seek you out. Please, Aresia. Don't throw your life away."

I sat down on the felled tree that served as the support base of the ark's framework. "Go, Japheth. Do not wait. Just go. Be with your family. Be . . . be with Neses. She loves you, and you know that. She will make a good wife."

He backed away, shaking his head, anger clouding his expression. He opened his mouth as if to speak, but found no words. His jaw snapped closed, and he whirled on a heel and marched away, anger in the hard lines of his posture.

I watched him walk away, and when he was gone I collapsed. Tears dripped down my chin as I watched him depart. I wanted to go with him, to cling to him, to tell him *I* loved him. But yet I knew if Noah discovered Japheth had snuck me aboard, irreparable damage would be done to their still-fragile relationship. Noah had always been clear about the numbers of humans who could go on this journey, and that number had never included me.

So, with tears in my eyes, I watched the animals climb aboard the ark, two by two, from the largest prowling lions and swaying, grumbling bears to the tiniest rabbits and pink-tailed mice. Insects whirred and hopped, wings coruscating in the intermittent flashes of lightning. Two by two, and two by two.

For hours, it continued. Behind me, the ark vibrated with noise, echoing with hoof clops and animal snarls.

Lightning streaked across the sky in a million blinding flashes, and thunder rolled incessantly, and beneath me the earth shook like a pebble in a child's cupped hands. Rain still dribbled intermittently, splats and splatters here and there, as if the sky was pregnant with rain, a woman nearing her time, labor pains lancing nonstop, the babe crowning, but the moment of birth not yet come.

Tension crackled. I felt it, felt my hairs standing on end, all along my arms and the back of my neck. Vibrations quaked under the soles of my feet, rumblings shivering in my belly. I looked up, and the sky was a seething black whirlpool, laced with lightning like cracks in the fabric of the sky.

I watched, and I watched, and finally, the last pair of creatures waddled aboard the ark, a giant fat pink sow and a hairy thick-tusked boar, their beady eyes glinting and their snorts coming quick and nervous.

Shem, Ham, Japheth, Zara, Neses, Sedele, and Ne'eletama were all aboard the ark long since. Only Noah and I remained outside.

Noah strode out into the meadow just beyond the ramp, now churned into mud. He stopped a dozen paces from the ramp, raised his arms to the sky, head tipped back, long silvering black hair blown horizontal in the raging wind, his beard flattened against his side and trailing under one arm. A bolt of lightning sizzled down from the heavens, striking the mud at Noah's feet. Another bolt struck behind him, and again to his left, and then his right.

Thunder crashed directly overhead, so loud and close my eardrums ached and my stomach tumbled inside me.

Again, and again, and again, lightning struck all around Noah, until the air around him was a blinding torus of purple-blue-white, pure fire, pure light. The thunder detonated, rattling my bones in my skin, booming and booming and booming.

I could just barely make out Noah's form inside the blazing ring of light, his arms stretched high over his head. He was at peace, unafraid. The thunder boomed in a rhythm, crashed in a syntactic pattern and became a voice.

A Voice.

His Voice.

I huddled against the side of the ark, weeping in abject terror, as the lightning seared and the thunder cracked and the whole earth shook, as if straining at the seams.

I heard the voice of El speaking in the howl of the wind, in the sizzle of the lightning, in the crash of the thunder, and I knew His Voice . . . but His words were not meant for me.

I heard Him, but I could not understand.

I wept, and I wept, and I wept.

After a time without measure, the lightning ceased to strike and to spin, the thunder faded into distant rumbles, and the presence of El receded.

Noah strode aboard the ark, his staff in his hands. He paused at the top of the ramp, and he cast his eyes down to where I hid, huddled against the belly of the ark.

He saw me.

His flesh radiated, the glory of El Shaddai staining his skin luminescent.

He saw me, and I felt the sorrow in his gaze. His eyes swept across the land, from east to west, and I thought perhaps his gaze saw all the lands and all the peoples therein, all the lives in the cities, all the souls awaiting their deaths.

In that moment, Noah saw them all, and his sorrow was for them. His gaze swept across the earth and came to rest once more upon me.

Now his sorrow was for me.

# CHAPTER 14

## The Windows of Heaven

"... On that day all the fountains of the great
deep burst forth, and the windows of the
heavens were opened." Genesis 7:11 (NLT)

A SINGLE CRACK OF THUNDER, SO LOUD MY EARS rang and I was rendered deaf.

In the moment of that peal of thunder, the skies opened. Heaven was cracked open upon the command of Elohim, and the rains descended. Rain so thick I could not see my hand in front of my face. Rain so dense, so hard, so fierce that the sound of the waters pouring from heaven was a roar so great and so mighty my bones shook from the violence.

The shaking from within the earth intensified, the ground rattling audibly, and the rumbling changed and deepened, the shaking became violent, and then ceased. The rains roared unending, but the rumbling from below had been so ever present for so many days that its absence was a deafening silence.

The quiet did not last for long.

The sound I heard then defies human language. It sent the ark to swaying on its supports, and the sound knocked me to the ground. It was a wall of noise, so all consuming, deafening, violent, and vengeful that I was compelled to flatten myself to the ground before it. All the earth heard it, then.

The shaking, the trembling, the rattling in the earth was gone, and now I heard a new sound, a new roaring, as of a lion prowling the floor of heaven, a lion so great it could swallow the earth in one gulp.

I cowered on the ground, waters rising around me, swirling around my ankles, wetting my belly with icy cold. I crouched, waiting, watching.

In the distance, I saw a mountain peak split open like a pebble dashed against a boulder, and from within the crack spat a column of water, spurting into the sky hundreds of cubits above the top of the peak. My gaze swept east, and I saw the earth shake and watched the ground itself crack apart, and a spray of water gush into the air with a roaring hiss. To the west, in the plains south of Umma, I saw a hundred such fountains pouring skyward from cracks in the earth.

The waters rose around me, until I was forced to stand. It passed my knees, rushing and eddying and swirling, the currents violent, tugging at me. The floodwaters lapped at the ark, slapping against the side, and I heard the mighty vessel groan and creak. I put my hand against the pitch-sticky side and felt it swaying as the waters rose.

My death approached.

Yet . . .

I looked up and saw the opening of the ark's great door, the ramp still lowered.

Lightning flashed, and the rains hammered down in a blinding deluge.

The floodwaters caught at my thighs, and I felt the final pangs of fear bite into me.

A new sound, then, yet another kind of rumbling, a bone-shaking roar, from the northeast, from the mountains thence. I peered through the gnashing, pelting, weltering wall of rain, and saw white. The ark shook, and the sky shook, and the ground shook, and I stared hard through the rain.

The whiteness was a wall of water. Rushing. Cascading. A flood, god-high—God-high. A flood that touched the sky itself, smashing against the hills and pouring over them, covering them.

I wept and saw my death approaching.

Of its own accord, the ramp ascended, pulled by

no ropes, pushed by no hands, guided by no man. It rose, trembling, creaking, and dripping floodwater.

I was covered to my waist, now, shivering, weeping, crying out loud to the Lord of Heaven, to Elohim, but my cries of torment were lost in the roaring of the approaching flood.

At the last, as the waters bore me upward, as the wall seethed toward me, I knew my weakness, and I knew my sin.

*Elohim, my Lord God El Shaddai . . . forgive me.*

I caught hold of the ramp as it ascended, the wood slick under my fingers.

# ARESIA'S SONG

The voices of my brothers
echo in the temples,
sandals stomping.
They swagger like bold heroes,
bellow like proud bulls;
they offer hollow sacrifices
to empty and silent gods,
hungry hands and selfish eyes
devouring all that they survey.
Their victims weep and plead to deaf ears,
and their laughter mocks the dying.
Sons of men and angels,
princes of the earth,
these brutal demi-gods
carve their names in shifting sand.
They do not see their demise
rushing down upon them
floodwaters from the mighty Tigris,
a deluge from the Euphrates.

I walk among the mortal men of the earth,
and I hear their prayers,
prayed not to gods many and futile,
but to The One God
whose Voice reverberates from the mountaintops.

I walk among them,
searching for a light
to illumine my darkened soul.
I have no sacrifice I can offer up,
no prayers to heal the wounds
inflicted by my father's fists,
by the King's anger.

The waters rise up,
the tides come and they cannot be stopped,
the waters drown my city,
and carry away my people,
tear down the ziggurat
and the palace.
The floodwaters of The One God
bathe me clean;
Elohim draws me to Himself
and stills my cry
with the comfort of rushing waters,
and I am silenced.